GET HAPPY

OTHER BOOKS BY MARY AMATO

YA

Guitar Notes

Middle Grade

Invisible Lines

The Naked Mole-Rat Letters

MARY AMATO

Get Happy

EGMONT
New York   USA

Hear the songs from the book, sing with the karaoke tracks,
and learn how to write your own songs on Mary Amato's website,
www.thrumsociety.com

EGMONT

We bring stories to life

First published by Egmont USA, 2014
443 Park Avenue South, Suite 806
New York, NY 10016

1 3 5 7 9 8 6 4 2

www.egmontusa.com
www.maryamato.com
Interior book design: Kathleen Westray
Cover design: Jeanine Henderson

Library of Congress Cataloging-in-Publication Data
Amato, Mary.
Get happy / Mary Amato.
pages cm
Summary: On her birthday, Minerva, a sixteen-year-old singer/songwriter, hears
from the father she has never known and her placid life is turned upside down.
ISBN 978-1-60684-522-6 (hardcover) – ISBN 978-1-60684-523-3 (eBook)
[1. Musicians–Fiction. 2. Families–Fiction. 3. Fathers and daughters–Fiction.
4. Friendship–Fiction.] I. Title.
PZ7.A49165Ge 2014
[Fic]–dc23
2014008736

Printed in the United States of America

For all my fans who send me such touching and heartfelt letters — your words, your voices inspire me to write and revise, even on the hardest of days.

CONTENTS

1

UGLY SWEATERS
& THE SHOCK
OF A LIFETIME

IT STARTS WITH the gift. Please don't judge me, but I could tell by the shape and size of the box that it wasn't a ukulele and I felt a little piece of my soul start to drown.

Maybe to you, a ukulele doesn't sound like a big deal, or maybe you think, hey, her mom got her that panini maker she begged for two years ago and she only used it once, but a ukulele is not a panini maker. You can't express your true emotions with panini.

So there I was on the morning of my birthday, with

my mom standing by the table, an excited little-kid look in her eyes. The dining room was decorated with fresh flowers, streamers, and balloons. Sixteen candles were dripping wax onto a huge, frosted cinnamon roll. We Watsons have a morning ritual for birthdays: a special breakfast and the opening of the gift right away — even if it falls on a school day. "Happy birthday, Minny!" she said, and then sang the birthday song.

Already knowing I hadn't gotten my wish, I closed my eyes and thought, *Deliver me from eternal misery,* and then I opened my eyes and blew out the flames.

She clapped and handed me her gift. "Open it!"

I took the box, my face muscles preparing a fake smile. "Beautiful wrapping job, Mom," I said. "It's too pretty to open."

She laughed.

Same routine every year.

Making sure not to damage the gift wrap — my mom is a big reuser of stuff — I opened it: a navy blue sweater with huge white snowflakes around the neck and the bottoms of the sleeves.

"You don't have any stylish cardigans," my mom

said, as if it were a crime. "And so I splurged on the real deal." She showed me the designer label.

"Wow," I said. "Thanks so much."

"You like it?"

"It's a really pretty design." My smile was twitching slightly at this point, which I believe is what happens when your soul is suffocating, but my mom didn't notice. She was whipping the sweater out of the box.

"Try it on. You can wear it today." She gave the outfit I was wearing one of her famous looks. The Pat Watson look. A mix of pity and disapproval with a dash of *Let me save* you thrown in. The dress I was wearing that day was my favorite, a green vintage raggedy thing I had found in the dollar box at the Goodwill store. The dollar box. I will be proud if I have a daughter who can put together a wardrobe for one buck. My mother, on the other hand, tries to quietly dispose of my sale items in the kitchen trash.

I put on the sweater.

"It's gorgeous." She clapped and then reached over, her eyes bright. "See . . . if you button it all the way up, it will look really pretty."

I buttoned it up.

"And a little something from your aunt!" My mom handed me a card.

Dear Minerva, old fogeys like me don't know what sixteen-year-olds want, so here's some dough. Spend it all in one place!

A nice, crisp twenty-dollar bill tucked inside.

I know there are children in the world who would be overjoyed to get a navy blue cardigan and a twenty-dollar bill. But I had put that picture of the uke on the fridge before Christmas — the store address and phone number circled with a bright blue highlighter. Hint, hint. And every time my friend Finnegan came over, he'd ooh and aah over the picture and say in front of my mom, "Minerva, this is so *you*. No wonder your soul will not feel complete until you have it." Hint, hint. (Finnegan, if you're reading this, thank you.)

Even though I knew it was small of me, I couldn't help being depressed that day. Let the record show that there were extenuating factors: The temperature was nineteen degrees Fahrenheit, with a wind chill factor of minus ten; my "extended constructed essay" on the social and economic pressures leading up to the Civil War was due; the audition that Fin was pressuring me to do was after school; and to top it off, the bottoms of my feet were itchy. I had put on these Dead Sea salt detox foot patches, documented in clinical studies to pull toxins out of the body, resulting in healthier skin, organs, cells, and even hair. They basically gave me hives.

The universe doesn't care if it's your birthday.

After breakfast, I stuffed my itchy feet into boots, suited up in all my winter gear, wound an extra scarf around my head, grabbed my backpack, and was hobbling to the door, when my mom said, "Wait! With all the excitement, we forgot to make lunch."

I groaned.

"Sit, birthday girl." She patted the top of my head. "What do you want — ham or peanut butter?"

"Peanut butter," I said. I sat on the edge of the coffee table, staring at the fake-embroidered sign that she had hung on the wall by the front door for Christmas and hadn't yet taken down. TIDINGS OF JOY!

I took off my mittens and pulled out my songwriting journal.

The day you're born
You start dying.
Why bother trying?
Don't light candles.
Don't make wishes.
Happy birthdays are fictitious.
Lick some frosting.
Eat some wax.

I was trying to think of a rhyme for *wax* when I heard footsteps crunching in the snow. I opened the door and was hit by a blast of dangerously cold, freeze-your-nose-off air, just as a FedEx guy was about to knock.

He handed me a small padded envelope and asked for a signature, his breath making puffs in the air. I was about to call for my mom, when I saw that it was addressed to Pat and Minerva Watson.

The return address was printed on the envelope — Shedd Aquarium — and, above that, K.C. had been written in black pen. K.C. were the initials of someone my mom and I never talked about, someone I hadn't seen since I was two years old: Kenneth Chip. My dad.

I signed, my heart pounding so loud I was sure it was going to burst right through my winter coat and sucker punch the FedEex guy off my front doorstep.

"Thank you." I tried sounding casual.

"Have a good one," the guy said, and left.

I closed the door.

"Did you just say something?" my mom called from the kitchen.

"No." Quickly, I stuffed the envelope into my backpack.

"Apple or clementine?" she called.

"Apple," I called back.

She walked in and handed me a lunch sack. "Ready to go, birthday girl?"

I nodded and shot off a natural-looking smile. "Ready."

2

FINNEGAN & THE PACKAGE

I saw Finnegan getting dropped off at school. He's on the short side for a guy, with a good build and lots of Irishy freckles; and in the winter, whenever he wears his green peacoat and goofy purple hat, he looks leprechauny. Even though he was the only person I could talk to, I confess I tried to beat him inside the building. He would want me to open the envelope, and I wasn't ready.

"Minerva, wait up!" he yelled. "Are yours working? I think my skin is glowing. Am I glowing?"

The detox foot patches had come four to a box and we had split the cost.

"They gave me hives." I hobbled in through the school doors. "We shouldn't have wasted our money."

"My feet itch, too," he said. "But I think it means they're working."

I headed down the hall. "I'm not doing the audition."

Fin followed. "Minerva, you promised. I'm not letting you chicken out. They'll stop itching. Why are you so grumpy? Oh! I almost forgot. Happy birthday!" He started punching my arm, our old ritual. "One, two, three, four —"

"Knock it off, Fin. I'm sick. I'm going to barf."

"Five, six, seven . . . you are fine. I have a present for you, and I'm going to give it to you as soon as you've received all sixteen punches . . . eight, nine —"

I slapped his arm away. "Fin, I got a FedEx envelope from somebody with the initials K.C."

"K.C." He stopped. "Your dad? Why didn't you tell me right away? What was in it?"

I headed for the bathroom.

"Minerva, what was in it?" Fin followed.

"I don't know. I don't even know if it's from him." I stopped, took off my mittens, and pulled the envelope out of my backpack. "I didn't tell my mom."

"Open it!" he practically screamed.

"Not here. Not now. If it's from him, I'll have to walk around enraged all day and I won't be able to do anything about it."

"Yes, here. Yes, now," he said. "If you don't open it, it'll be worse."

We stood still as the crowd surged through the hallway in both directions, Fin's eyes soft and locked on mine, his goofy purple hat sticking up. He was right. I pushed open the girls' bathroom door. "Wait for me in case I faint. If you hear a clunk, come in."

"Totally not fair," Fin called out. "Open it out here."

The girls' bathroom was hot and smelled like a porta-potty. Even though the room was empty, I squeezed into a stall with my winter gear still on, and locked the door. I stared at the printed return address: the Shedd Aquarium, the big aquarium in Chicago that I went to on a field trip in the second grade and loved, the place I used to beg my mom to take me back to see again.

The initials K.C. were printed carefully, neatly, on the FedEx line for sender name. This K.C. obviously worked for the aquarium, so I figured the envelope couldn't be from my dad. I had always assumed he lived in some trailer park in Kansas or Idaho or Nevada or some faraway place. In my mind, he was a hedonistic loser, a druggie, an alcoholic, and a convict all rolled into one, and that's why my mom never talked about him and why I had never heard from him. I knew only three things about him: He and my mom met when he had a temporary job in Chicago, he had "Pacific island" genes, and he left us, never paying any child support. My blue-eyed, once-blond mother offered up only those tidbits years ago when I got the nerve to ask how I ended up with the blackest hair and darkest eyes of any white girl in Evanston, Illinois. End of conversation.

I opened the envelope and pulled out a cream-colored note card. The paper was expensive, elegant, with the initials K.C. embossed on the front, and nothing else.

Pat,

Enclosed is a birthday gift for Minerva. I am hoping that you and Minerva will talk about it and come to the decision that we should at least meet now that I'm nearby. I am more than willing to talk about concerns or issues at length over the phone. It's time, Pat.

KC

The bathroom walls began to blur. I slipped the card into my backpack and then I pulled a small box out of the FedEx envelope. Another card, which was under the box, fluttered out — heading for the toilet too fast to grab. My heart almost stopped. Miraculously, it landed on the toilet seat. One small breeze and it would be floating in somebody else's pee. In slow motion, I leaned down, keeping my head back and my chin up so my scarf wouldn't knock it in. Gingerly, I lifted it from the seat.

Finnegan's voice from the hallway: "Minerva! Come out!"

The temperature in that bathroom must have been a hundred and twenty degrees. Little beads of sweat prickled my forehead.

Dear Minerva,
    Happy sixteenth birthday. What do I say?

Every time I sit down to write, I wonder if my
words will be welcome.

    Now that you're sixteen, I'm hoping you
might have more of an interest in getting to
know me. I'd love to learn more about you. Are
you into sports? Art? Do you play an instrument?

    Enclosed is a little something. I know that
gifts are a far cry from being there all these
years, but I want you to know that I am always
thinking about you. I don't know if it's your
style, but I hope you like it.

                    Love, your dad

I broke out in a full sweat. Inside the box, nes-
tled on a little cotton bed, was a large sterling silver
pendant, a seahorse, suspended from a black silk cord.
A seahorse. It was beautiful, the spine studded with
small black pearls, the tail reaching up to curl around
the cord. Classy and hip. A seriously legitimate work
of art.

Fin's voice: "Minerva? Is anybody else in there? If
anybody's in there, this is your warning. I'm coming
in."

Sweat was dripping down my neck, under my hat, and under my arms. My lungs felt like heavy sponges. I pushed open the stall door just as Fin was coming in.

"So?" he asked.

I put the box and cards in my backpack, threw the FedEx envelope into the trash, and walked out.

He followed. "Let it out, Minerva. Talk to me."

I kept walking, yanking off my scarf and hat.

"Minerva . . ." He grabbed my arm.

"It's him," I said, pulling my arm out of my coat.

"What did he say? What was in there? Minerva! That is a truly hideous sweater. You got it from Pat, didn't you? She made you wear it?" His face fell. "Aw, you didn't get the ukulele, did you?"

I stopped. "He gave me a necklace." I pulled out the box and opened it.

"It's gorgeous. It's a seahorse! You love seahorses. Remember, I gave you that seahorse jewelry box for your birthday? We were, like, seven. This looks so expensive!" His voice was gleeful.

He was about to take it out, but I put the lid on and gave him a withering look. "I have hated his guts as far back as I can remember. He left when I was two. Am I supposed to forgive him because he suddenly gives me some jewelry? This just makes me hate him even more."

"Look at it this way. He owes you big-time, and this is a start."

"I don't want it."

"Sell it and buy your uke with it."

"I'm not buying my uke with his money. It'll have bad juju. I don't want anything to do with him."

Fin tugged my arm. "Please tell me you're going to benefit financially from this."

I bolted toward my locker.

"Sorry, Minerva. Was there a letter?" He followed, picking up my coat, which was dragging on the floor.

I stopped, and he tried to give me a hug, but I pulled away and went to my locker. He followed, trying to get me to talk. I stuffed in all my outerwear — including the sweater — and then took off to class.

He called after me. "Wait!"

I turned.

He pulled a notebook-size gift out of his backpack and handed it to me. "We can talk about it after school. Come to the audition. It'll take your mind off all this."

The gift was wrapped in a hilarious old poster of

SpongeBob, and he gave it with a smile so sweet I had to look away. I turned, ran into my first-period classroom, sat down, and unwrapped the present. A book. *Ukulele Love: How to Play Big Songs on a Tiny Instrument.*

I choked back a sob, and a gurgle came out.

"What's her problem?" Rick Rogan, the idiot who sat next to me, asked.

"She's sad because the Ugly Club elected someone else as president," his idiot friend said.

Yep. People are mean.

3

THE AUDITION

I DON'T KNOW if you've ever experienced a psychological trauma, but one of the strangest things about it is that your body continues to operate. When you get emotionally overwhelmed, it would be nice if your body went into a temporary coma so you could have time to process everything. Instead, you get earth-shattering news and you have to walk to class, sit in a chair, take a pop quiz, breathe, swallow.

I went through the day with the necklace sitting in the bottom of my backpack like a small beautifully crafted silver bomb. Finally, school ended and Finnegan grabbed me and marched me out the door into the cold January air.

"I know you're upset, Minerva, but we're going to this audition. You promised."

I stopped. "It's my birthday, Fin, and I've been traumatized. I want to go to your house and watch *SpongeBob*. Maybe get some sushi —"

He gave me a look. "You're not thinking clearly. All this Kenneth Chip stuff has hijacked your brain. This is our one and only chance to audition for the Get Happy job, which would be a good thing for both of us to get."

"I'm not an auditioner, Fin. You are."

"You are an amazing singer, Minerva."

"With you. Or in chorus or in the shower, not at an audition."

He pulled me along. "Okay. You can buy a ukulele with your first paycheck. Just think of that. And after the audition, you can come over and we'll do some research on Kenneth Chip, and if we discover that he's rich, then you're going to deal with your rage by milking him for millions of dollars. If he were my dad, I'd get him to pay for new shoes, clothes, a new phone. You should demand a weekly allowance."

"I can't audition. I can't focus on anything. I haven't

even figured out how I'm going to tell my mom about this."

"See? That's why you should come. At least walk with me and then you can decide once you get there." He pulled a can out of his backpack. "Ginger and ginseng energy drink," he said. "This will give you vigor and vim."

My first laugh of the day. "Is *vim* a word?"

"Yes. It means 'robust energy and enthusiasm.'" He popped it open. "Oooh! Serious fizz!" He took a sip and then gagged.

"Bad?" I asked.

"No, it's good," he said, trying to regain control of his face.

My second laugh of the day. Fin doesn't believe in having regrets, so he likes everything he buys.

I took a sip. It tasted like carbonated tea steeped in battery acid.

We passed the can back and forth as we negotiated the sidewalk. The snow that hadn't been properly shoveled had turned into treacherous patches of ice.

"Come on, people, some of us have to walk out here," Fin shouted to no one. "Shovel your sidewalks!"

Our high school is about five blocks from down-town Evanston, so it didn't take us long to get there, even with the ice and my itchy-foot zombie walk. On the corner of Grove and Sherman, Fin pulled out the flyer and double-checked the address.

"This is it. Sixth floor," Fin said, and we both looked up at the tall white building.

"I've walked by this corner a million times, so why haven't I noticed this?" I asked.

"Because it's probably filled with podiatrists and old people getting their warts removed." He held open the door.

I didn't move.

"Just come up with me. If you don't, I'm telling Pat that you murdered your new sweater." He pulled me into the lobby and pushed the elevator button. "Energy is oozing through my veins. It's the vim and vigor juice!" He squealed in the funniest way and I started laughing, which made him laugh.

I stopped. "Fin, your tongue is gray. Is mine?" In the reflection of the elevator doors, we examined our tongues.

"Zut alors!" he said. "That juice was probably made of endangered elephant-butt skin!"

We both started cracking up.

"They won't hire us!" he wailed.

"They cannot discriminate on the basis of tongue color," I said. "That is totally illegal."

The elevator arrived. As we got in, another guy ran into the lobby and asked us to hold it.

It's impossible to know everybody in our high school, especially people who are not in our actual grade level or people who didn't go to our middle school, but I recognized this guy because he was in the school's jazz ensemble, and we see those guys when we have chorus-band concerts.

"You play that big gigantic thing, right?" Fin was using his flirty voice. He uses it on everybody — grocery store clerks, cheerleaders, hot guys waiting in line at the movies, old ladies with thick glasses, puppies . . . you name it.

"It's called a bass, Finnegan," I said.

"A double bass, actually," the guy said. "I'm Hayes Martinelli."

Formal introductions are not exactly common among high school people. Usually, you get to know new people gradually because you sit next to them in class, so I was shocked when he stuck his hand out in this old-fashioned way with this deliberate eye-to-eye gaze and said, "Hello, Minerva."

I shook his hand, which was strange.

(Hayes, if you're reading this, I didn't mean that your hand felt weird. I will admit here that your hand actually felt nice — cold from the air, but not like a robot or a frozen fish fillet — and, if you recall, we actually connected in this perfect, smooth move without banging thumbs or squashing pinkies. Olympic judges would've given the handshake ten out of ten. What was strange was suddenly feeling a naked palm against my own naked palm because, to be honest, at the time, I didn't go around shaking guys' hands and also maybe because so much of our skin is covered up in the wintertime. It was also surprising to hear you say, "Hello, Minerva," because I had no idea you knew who I was.)

While I was reeling from this, Hayes reached over and shook Finnegan's hand. And Fin looked dazed and amazed by the whole thing, too.

"Sorry. It's a reflex," Hayes said. "I come from a handshaking family."

"It's debonair," Fin said, and pushed the button for the sixth floor. "I'm going to shake hands with the Get Happy people. What floor do you want?"

"Seven," Hayes said. "Floor number seven."

Fin punched the button. "Podiatrist?"

"Podiatrist? No, actually," Hayes said, "I have an appointment with a dimpiatrist."

I wasn't sure what that was, so I glanced at Fin, who looked equally clueless.

"I'm getting my dimples removed," Hayes said. Perfectly straight face.

Fin and I laughed.

The metallic elevator doors in this building were like a spy tool. As they closed, our reflections appeared, so I could secretly check out Hayes. Tall, skinny, no hat, curly hair, ears and nose red from the cold, a vintage-looking wool coat, nice choice, and a slightly goofy but intense smile on his face, as if he were telling himself a really important joke. Just the right size dimples. He noticed my gaze in the reflection, and I quickly looked at the small numbers lighting up along the top of the elevator. B1, B2, B3. Next to me, Fin was doing his bouncy thing. He's hyper to begin with, and the energy drink was making it worse.

"Um, I think we're going down," Hayes said.

I wanted to reply with some witty banter. "Yeah," I said. Brilliant.

The doors opened to a parking garage.

Fin pushed the 6 button again and again and then again.

As the doors closed, Hayes said, "You're both in chorus."

"We are," Fin said. "We're chorus geeks."

Then the most amazing thing happened. Hayes turned to me and told me that he happened to be walking behind the school last week and Fin and I were there, taking the shortcut to Park Place, and he heard me sing. "You were singing a song," he said, "and one of the lines was 'I'll play a tiny violin and commit only tiny sins.'"

"She made that up!" Fin elbowed me. "You have a fan." He turned to Hayes. "Are you stalking her?"

Hayes laughed and blushed slightly. "I like songs with unexpected lyrics."

"See, Minerva, he likes your song."

I bowed.

Fin elbowed me again. "I keep telling you that your songs are good." He added to Hayes, "I keep telling her she should do open mics."

I do what I always do when I am nervous: I turn

into a ridiculous clown. I sang a line from my song really high and really off-key: *"I will play a tiny violin and commit only tiny sins and all my troubles will be small. . . ."*

Hayes laughed. "Keep going."

I shut up. As they say in showbiz, better to leave them wanting more.

"Do you play a tiny violin?" he asked.

"No, but she wants a uke," Fin said.

"A uke?" he asked.

"I've always liked tiny things."

When we finally got to the sixth floor, Fin said, "Ditch the dimpiatrist or wherever you're going and come with us. We're auditioning to be entertainers at parties for kids."

Hayes looked at me.

"I know," I said. "It's absurd."

Hayes shrugged. "Okay, I'm in."

"You're kidding!" I exclaimed.

"Getting a job is on my list of things to do," he said.

Maybe it was the vim and vigor juice . . . maybe it was the fact that I didn't want to go home . . . maybe it was inspiring to see Hayes, who I had pegged as the quiet type, saying yes. . . . I decided to go for it, too.

The Get Happy office looked like a preschool: one big, open room, each wall painted in a different bright color, a dozen pillows in a circle in the center of the carpeted floor. A row of costumes hung along one wall, giant plastic tubs labeled PROPS lined another wall, and curtained dressing rooms and a desk were toward the back.

"If they make me sing 'The Wheels on the Bus,' I will throw myself under one," I whispered to Fin. Hayes heard it and laughed.

"Welcome! Come in!" A woman jumped up from behind the desk and came out to greet us, carrying a clipboard. A younger version of my mom, the kind of woman who loves coupons, whose fingernails always shine, whose hair is coiffed instead of cut. "I'm Joy Banks, manager of the brand-new Evanston branch of Get Happy. You're here for the auditions? Come in."

Fin whipped off his purple hat, marched up, and shook her hand. Hayes and I exchanged a smile and stepped up with the charm, too.

After hanging up coats and filling out forms, we sat in the circle on the floor, the empty pillows screaming a silent accusation: *Nobody wants to work for your company.*

"Are we the only ones?" Fin asked.

The woman's smile stretched like a rubber band. "So far."

Just then the door opened and we all turned.

A tall, gorgeous girl walked in, a cross between a young Halle Berry and Rihanna, but totally natural. Huge dark eyes with dark lashes, great cheekbones, glossy lips. Her long hair pinned up in a messy and unbelievably pretty way. She was wearing a short skirt with black boots and bare thighs and, over it, a big loose guy's jacket, like the winter had caught her off guard, and her boyfriend had given her his jacket. "Hi." She waved with a blinding smile.

"This is why I hate auditions," I whispered to Finnegan.

The girl took off the jacket, her exotic bangle bracelets jangling, to reveal a tight V-neck T-shirt. Hayes was checking her out. Really, I don't understand how some girls get their arms and legs to look so Hollywood, a combination of the perfect shape — actual muscles — and polished-looking, goddesslike, hairless skin. My legs and arms don't have a shape, and no matter how often I shave my legs, the skin never looks right. It's one thing I actually like about winter: You can wear long sleeves and leggings every day.

"Welcome, welcome!" Joy said, clearly relieved to see someone who actually looked like a potential star walking through the door. "You can fill out forms later. Sit down! Join us!"

As the new girl did one of those model-type moves, somehow sitting down in a miniskirt so the guys couldn't see up it, Joy launched in, a fake gleam in her heavily made-up eyes. "Let's introduce ourselves. Just tell us your name, why you're here, a tidbit or two about yourself and your hobbies, and one thing you're good at. Ladies first." She gestured to the other girl to start.

The girl waved again. "Hi. My name is Cassie Lott. I'm here because I really want to get a job of my own and I like parties."

Hayes and Fin and Joy all laughed.

She went on. "I go to the Parker School in Chicago. Let's see . . . I love kids and I do a lot of volunteer work on my breaks. I'm on the dance team and am in chorus. I'd say my main hobby is diving." She smiled. "I have a blog about it." She did this nose-crinkling smile. "Did I forget something or is that enough?"

Joy's face almost exploded with excitement. "Wonderful!"

Hired. Really. Why bother with the charade of an audition? A singing, dancing, athletic girl! I could just see her five years from now, standing on the platform in her swimsuit, getting the gold medal and then giving it to charity and appearing on the cover of *Vogue*.

"Next?" Joy looked at me.

The tension of the day opened a valve, and the acidic juices of my inner nature surged out. "My name is Minerva Watson." I smiled. "I'd love to be part of the Get Happy family! I sing, and dance, and act, and twirl batons at Evanston High School. And I volunteer at Children's Hospital, the animal shelter, and a homeless center."

Joy put one hand over her heart, completely buying it. "That is so sweet."

Fin snorted back a laugh, but I kept smiling and staring at Joy.

"And what about you?" She turned to Fin.

"I'm Finnegan O'Connor." There was that flirty voice again. "I go to EHS with Minerva. I do lots of shows and I love to sing — "

"His voice is amazing," I offered.

He smiled, and then he took a big breath like he was excited to be alive, and started gushing. "I love entertaining. I love being in the spotlight and I really know how to work a crowd. I think birthdays should be full of vigor and vim, and I think Get Happy is such a great idea for a company."

I was biting my bottom lip so hard I thought it was going to bleed.

"Thank you," Joy said. "Yes, birthdays should be fun. I love your enthusiasm." Joy turned to Hayes next, who threw us an amused look.

"My name is Hayes Martinelli. To be honest, I heard about this today and thought I'd check it out." He shrugged.

"Hobbies?" Joy asked.

"I play the double bass and lately I've been recording original stuff. Jazz."

"I love jazz," Cassie said.

"Wonderful, Hayes!" Joy exclaimed. "Isn't that

rewarding?" You could tell she didn't give a flying fig about jazz. "Well, it looks like we have some real Get Happy material here." Joy pulled scripts out of a file cabinet. Fin got pirate, Hayes got cowboy, Cassie got princess, and I got mermaid.

Fin shrieked when he saw mine, and started quoting our favorite *Little Mermaid* lines because I had a childhood obsession with Ariel.

Joy spoke up. "These are generic characters because of the whole copyright issue. You'll see in your scripts. Let's just go around the circle and each read the first page. Just try to get into character."

We all took turns reading. I tried to think like a half fish, half girl and didn't do too terribly. Hayes looked clueless when it was his turn, but helpful Cassie squeezed his arm and told him to relax, to which Joy said, "Isn't that nice? And so true. Nobody here will bite you!"

Singing next. Fin sang first, and he belted it out without a shred of self-consciousness. He just doesn't care what anybody else thinks, which makes him very lovable, in my opinion. Then Cassie sang, and she was completely intimidating. She's got The Voice.

I had to go on after that. My voice came out mousy,

which is what happens when I'm nervous. I got mad at myself because I could do better and now I really wanted the job and I was afraid I wasn't going to get it. Even Hayes was more confident. Finally, the whole ordeal was over, and the four of us left.

"Well, that was a hoot and a half," Fin said. "Full of vigor and vim."

Cassie laughed and put her arm around him. "You guys are hilarious. Thanks so much for telling me about this, Fin."

I stopped.

Fin gave me a guilty smile. "Cassie was in that hip-hop workshop I took at Soul to Sole over winter break," he explained.

I could've strangled him. I turned and gave him a private *thanks for inviting the competition* glare.

"All you guys did great," she said, giving Hayes's shoulders a squeeze. "I'm sure you'll make it."

Obviously regretting the fact that he had set me up for failure, Fin put his arm in mine and said: "It's Minerva's birthday. We have to sing!" Cassie and Hayes joined in, singing on the elevator ride down.

As we got out, Hayes said, "Wait. You need a

present." He reached into his jeans pocket and pulled out a dime, a ticket stub, and a small flat stone, the kind you find at the lake. He put the stone into the palm of my hand. "Happy birthday."

I smiled. "Gosh, you shouldn't have."

Cassie laughed.

We all headed out the front doors into a blast of freezing cold air. "It's not just a stone," he said. "It's a . . . plate for tiny cakes."

"A tiny cake plate?"

"Yes, it's called a . . . plakette," he said. "To go with your tiny violin and everything."

Laughing, Cassie reached over with her slender fingers, bracelets jangling, and snatched the stone. "Aw, I had a Barbie dollhouse with tiny plates and tiny cakes." Her heel hit an icy patch on the sidewalk and she slipped, grabbing Hayes to catch her balance. The stone flew out of her hand, was lit for a brief second by the gleam of the building's landscaping floodlight, and then disappeared into a two-foot pile of snow that had been shoveled against a bush.

An awkward silence. I could see the tiny shadowy depression left in the snow precisely where the stone had fallen through, and I was about to dig down through the snow to rescue it.

"I'm so sorry!" she said. "I hope it didn't have sentimental value or anything?"

Hayes laughed and waved the whole thing off. It was just a joke, ha-ha. We all laughed. Ha, ha, ha. Not wanting to look foolish, I left the stone in its snowy grave.

Cassie pulled keys out of her purse. "Anybody need a ride?"

I wanted to say I don't take rides from people who snatch birthday gifts, no matter how small, from other people's hands, but I kept my mouth shut while Hayes and Fin both said yes at the same time.

The sun had gone down and the temperature had dropped with it.

"We *all* want a ride," Fin said, looking at me pointedly, shivering. I tried to give him a look back, but he was already getting into the car. "Come on, Minerva."

I love Fin, but he tends to put comfort above principles. I pretended that I wanted to walk — even though the Dead Sea salt itch was still working its way out the bottoms of my feet — and headed off before anybody could see my face.

I walked a block, composing a new song in my head.

> *Drive on by. I'm fine.*
> *I don't mind being*
> *Left on the side of the road.*
> *I'd rather be cold*
> *Than go with your flow.*
> *Can't throw away my soul—*
> *It'll sink like a stone.*

When I opened my backpack to take out my songwriting journal, I saw the box with the necklace and the cards, and an angry black thundercloud of vermin, locusts, and murderous rage flew out.

The Kenneth Chip storm followed me all the way home.

4

MOM

"Where were you? I've been worried." My mother pounced. "You didn't answer your phone."

"Fin took me to Pan Asia Café for my birthday." The first in a string of lies.

"But I'm cooking a special dinner."

"I only had sushi. I'm still hungry." I stomped the snow off my boots, took off my coat, tried to smile, and told her I was going upstairs to get one little piece of homework done so I could relax.

"Where's your sweater?" she asked.

I looked down at my green dress. "Oh . . . I left it in my locker. It was really hot in my last class.

I think the heater was stuck in the high position or something."

She smiled. "Well, take good care of it. That is an expensive sweater, sweetie."

"Yep. Will do."

I didn't tell her about the audition because I figured I wouldn't make it and didn't want her to worry in advance — she would assume Get Happy was a scam — and I had no idea how to bring up the fact that my dad had sent the gift, because she would freak. Little lies buy a little time.

As I took my backpack up to my room, my phone buzzed. Text from Fin. **Call me!**

He started talking as soon as I called. "I'm sorry about the Cassie thing, but you did really good, and I think we're all — "

"Fin, I can't talk about this," I whispered. "I'm freaking out."

"Why? You're going to make it!"

"Not about that. About this whole Kenneth Chip thing."

"I can't believe I forgot about that!" he said. "I'm sorry. Hold on. . . . I'm getting my laptop."

"Wait, Fin — "

He came back on. "I'm going to the Shedd Aquarium Web site. . . ."

I closed my eyes. "No. Don't. I don't want to know."

"Hold on. . . . Here's the staff page. . . . Nobody is popping up for Kenneth Chip. I don't think he works there. Or if he does, he's not important enough to be listed."

"He's probably a custodian," I said. "He probably empties the trash bags."

"Hold on. . . . I'm Googling 'Kenneth Chip and Chicago.' . . . Nothing." He went on. "There's a Kenneth Chip in Orlando . . . a plumber. . . . Wait, it's Kenneth Chip Hanson. I think Chip is his nickname — "

"Dinner's ready!" my mom called.

I told Fin to stop looking and said good-bye. I slipped the cards and necklace into the toe of this funky sheepherder-type boot that was under my bed. My mother wouldn't touch that with a broom. Yes, when your mom has 24/7 access to your room, you have to be creative about where you hide things.

~

THAT WHOLE EVENING, I acted as if nothing were wrong, but after midnight, I crept downstairs into the dark kitchen. I remember the feeling in the air: It was as if the silence were a person in the room who was watching.

I turned on the computer and searched the Shedd Aquarium Web site. On the staff page, a dozen names were listed with their job titles, a short bio, and a photo after each name. *Jane Doe, President*, etc.

And then I got to this name — *Keanu Choy* — and I started having trouble breathing. The photo was a close-up of a guy treading water in a turquoise ocean, wearing scuba gear, smiling up at the camera, flawless brown skin, shining black hair, dark glittering almond-shaped eyes, a man who looked completely satisfied with his life. *VP Global Field Experiences and Director of SOS Project. Originally from Hawaii, Dr. Choy began his distinguished career with Shedd as an intern, just seventeen years ago. Specializing in the study of seahorses, he went on to found the Save Our Seahorse (SOS) Project. The Shedd Aquarium is delighted to be the new home of the SOS Project and to have Dr. Choy back on staff.*

The hair, the eyes, the seventeen years ago, the seahorses.

I sat there in the dark, staring at his photo while the

refrigerator hummed and the house slept. Eventually, I texted Fin, but of course he was sleeping, too.

~

THE NEXT MORNING, I woke in a numb, exhausted fog. There was my mom drinking coffee at the sink, chattering about how much she liked the new color scheme at Crate & Barrel, which is where she works, and there I was, trying to pack my lunch, not knowing how to bring up the whole father subject. Then I noticed the bag of potato chips on the pantry shelf and blurted casually: "So I wonder where Kenneth Chip is these days?"

She dropped her coffee cup. With a crash, it hit the tile floor and shattered, coffee spraying the white cabinets.

"Why did you say that?" she asked, the panic on her face as obvious as the mess.

We stared at each other, not moving. It was as if I had pulled her to the edge of a cliff, and I was afraid that if I answered truthfully, it would be like shoving her off.

"I just saw the chips and it popped into my head." It wasn't a total lie. It wasn't a total truth, either. I grabbed a paper towel and started wiping up.

"Be careful, Minny!" She pulled my hand away and grabbed a sponge. Her hand was shaking. "I have no idea where your father is and there's no need whatsoever to talk about that." She carefully pushed pieces of the cup into a pile. "He is not worth the time of day." She pulled the trash can over, started lifting the bigger pieces into it, and asked without looking: "It popped into your head because of the chips?"

"Yeah," I said quickly. "Just now."

She glanced at me. "Your father is not a nice person. If you let him in, he will hurt you. Promise me you will put him out of your mind."

I nodded.

"Good." She took a breath and stared at the splattered cabinets. "It's staining. Go get the cleanser from the bathroom, the green one with bleach in it. We can get this clean."

5

COWARDICE
& SNOOPING

Fin and I sat on the concrete bench by the flag-pole. We had only a few minutes before school started.

"Tell me everything," he said. He blew into his bare hands to warm them up. "Did you show her the necklace?"

"No. Her brain would have exploded. She freaked at the mere mention of his name. And I think she's lying about it."

"What do you mean?"

I took a breath, the cold air slicing into my lungs. I explained about the Web site and discovering Keanu Choy. "He's a Hawaiian seahorse expert."

"Hawaiian?"

"I have the same hair and eyes." Unfortunately, not the same skin.

"Hawaiian! I always thought you were half Japanese for some reason, but Hawaiian makes sense. Remember when we watched *Lilo and Stitch*, I said you looked like Lilo? Keanu Choy. I want that name. He sounds rich and exotic and cool."

A bus pulled up and a load of annoyingly loud freshmen got out. I closed my eyes and pressed my mittened hands against them. "You don't get it, Fin. He can't be cool. Either she lied about his name to keep me from finding him, or else his name was Kenneth Chip and he changed it to Keanu Choy."

"Why would he change his name?"

"I don't know. To avoid paying child support?"

"Maybe he was a bad person, but he's had a change of heart now. Maybe he was walking to work one day and God spoke to him from a burning shrub and said, 'Contact your daughter, dude!'"

"He doesn't walk to work. He sails."

"Okay," Fin laughed. "God spoke to him from a burning whale." He put his arm around me, and we sat for a few seconds, both of us cold, staring at a black crusted pile of snow at the edge of the sidewalk. "Let's assume his name has always been Choy, and your mom lied to you about it. Maybe she lied because he's great and she was afraid that you'd want to live with him in Hawaii! That makes sense." He grabbed my mitteny hands. "If you move to Hawaii, I'm going to kill you. Wait. . . . He works at the Shedd. So he lives here now? You have to go and meet him!"

My head was splitting open. "No. I don't want anything to do with him. He is a horrible, selfish person. I mean, who dumps a two-year-old kid and a wife?"

"What — exactly — did his letter say?"

I took a breath and recited it.

Fin's eyes were huge. "You memorized it."

"I read it a hundred times last night."

His eyes softened. "Min, he sounds nice."

"No. You should've heard my mom. 'Let him in and he will hurt you,' she said. He's a loser. I wish he was a drug addict. It would be better that way."

"How would that be better?"

"Because drug addicts are sick. They're basically ruled by the drugs. They make involuntary mistakes because their brains are addled."

"But it's better this way because you can get something out of him."

I looked at my boots.

The vice principal walked out, eyeballing us and the other vagrants who didn't want to go inside. "School is starting, people. You have thirty seconds."

Fin stood up and pulled me off the bench. "You have no real proof that Keanu Choy is your dad, Minerva. Your mom reacted to the name Kenneth Chip. You have this hunch . . . so let's go to Keanu Choy's office at the aquarium. You can say, 'Hi, are you my daddy?' If he is, then get everything you can from him and dump him. Protect yourself. You want money from him. That's it. Be practical. You don't want love. You just want cold hard cash."

My feet had stopped itching, but my toes were so cold they burned. "I'm not going to do that, Fin." We walked into school.

"Then confront your mom," he said. "Just lay it out on the table. 'Mother dearest, why have you been trying to convince me that I am related to a potato-based snack food?'"

~

FIN WAS RIGHT about the fact that I needed proof, but I couldn't get the nerve to talk to my mom that night. Instead, I barricaded myself in my room. I had all this emotion inside me that wanted to come out, and I was dying to write a song. That's how it works with me. When I'm emotional, it's like a song is inside me, and if I can just pull the song out, the anxiety and anger and pain flow out, too. But I was ukeless, and that made me more frustrated and angry.

I got out the uke songbook Fin had given me and decided to learn some chords, but it was hard without something physical to put my fingers on. Finally, I got a ruler, covered it with masking tape, drew lines on it with a permanent marker to look like the frets and strings on the neck of a uke, and attached it to a cookie tin with duct tape. A handy-dandy DIY practice uke.

I sat down with it and made the shapes of the chords on the neck with my left hand while I strummed against the cookie-tin part with my right hand, singing along.

Okay. Truly pathetic.

~

SOMEHOW, I GOT through the night, and I woke up the next morning, Saturday, to find a note on the kitchen counter from my mom: *Getting haircut and bagels.*

If you don't have the nerve to confront, then at least you can snoop, I said to myself.

One by one, I went through my mother's dresser drawers. Nothing. I wasn't even sure what I was looking for — photos, official documents . . . anything that might help me find proof of my dad's identity.

I scanned the photo albums in the bookshelf by my mom's bed. She had one for every year, starting with the year of my birth. I flipped through each page of the first two books, even though I knew there weren't any pictures of my dad in them. I'd gone through a phase, when I was eight, when I ripped a page out of an L. L. Bean catalogue, picturing a fatherly looking, black-haired guy sitting by a fireplace, and tried to convince myself it was him. I'd kept it under my pillow until, one day, I came home to find clean sheets and no trace of Mr. Bean.

I opened my mom's closet. Pink plastic storage boxes were stacked on the shelf above the clothes rack, all labeled in her neat handwriting. CDS. COSMETICS. DVDS. EYEGLASSES. GIFT CARDS. HAIR SUPPLIES.

OFFICE SUPPLIES. I opened the boxes, careful to put them back exactly where I found them, not finding any surprises. Big storage containers were under the bed, one labeled FALL/WINTER QUILTS — empty now — and the other labeled SPRING/SUMMER BEDSPREADS, which had our lightweight blankets in it. Clearly, if my mother ever lost her job, she could get one as a professional closet organizer. I peeked between the stored bedspreads, just to make absolutely sure nothing was hidden there.

"What are you doing?" My mom was standing in the doorway.

Talk about shock. I tried to smile innocently. "I didn't hear you come up. I was looking for my red sweater." I slid the storage box back under the bed. "I wanted to wear it, but it's not in my room."

"I don't store sweaters under there. Your room is a disaster, Minny. It's no wonder you can't find anything."

"Did you get bagels?" I asked to change the subject.

"Yes." She glanced at herself in the mirror.

"Yum. Thanks, Mommy. Hey, your coif looks great. Nice color."

Her face perked up. "Thank you, honey. That was nice of you to notice."

A horribly cheap trick — throw a compliment at your mom to make her go away.

~

Who am I?

I thought I had a clue.

Now I find someone new

Is hiding in my DNA.

What's a girl to do?

Call Nancy Drew?

Become a spy?

Hire a private eye?

Call the FBI?

Reply or say good-bye?

Cut the ties

And everything that implies?

Does someone

Who denied my life

Deserve a second try?

It's a twisted staircase

I have to climb,

A twisted staircase

Inside my mind.

6

GETTING THE JOB
& MAKING
A DECISION

"YOU JUST NEED one little thing to hold on to and you can get through the day."

That's something my aunt Joan said. One year when she and my uncle George were visiting his family, half their ranch in Colorado got swept away in a mudslide. My mom and I went out to help with the cleanup. I remember the smell of the damaged house, damp and moldy, and how sad it was because so much of Aunt Joan's stuff was ruined. She's a quilter, and her bedroom and sewing room had both collapsed, with everything in those rooms just sliding down the mountain. On our second day there, we discovered a plastic box that had somehow stayed watertight. When she opened it and saw scraps of fabric she had been saving to make a new quilt, she said that quote about needing one thing to hold on to and cried. Watsons don't cry in front of people, so the moment was seared into my brain.

I was remembering it because that Sunday, Joy Banks called and offered me a job at Get Happy, which gave me something to hold on to. The call came while I was in the bathroom, just getting out of the shower.

"Aren't you happy?" Joy asked.

"Absolutely. Thanks." The relief felt sweet, all the way down to the soles of my wet, itch-free feet.

"I know this is all very quick, but the first gigs are February second. I'll send an email with your training packet and your script attached. Print everything out. I'm hoping to have our training session next Saturday. Can you make it?"

I wiped the steam off the mirror. Minerva Watson was going to be an actual employee. Get Happy, Incorporated, was going to pay me to make parties fun. I smiled. Employment looked good on me.

"Can you make it?" she asked again.

"Yes, I'd be delighted," I said with a new professional lilt in my voice.

"Excellent. Welcome to the Get Happy family. Look for the details in your email, okay?"

"Okay. Wait! Who else made it from the audition?"

"Actually, I'm adding all four of you to the roster. I'm calling Finnegan O'Connor next."

I dried my hair and put together a genius outfit — employment is inspirational! — waiting to call Fin until I thought Joy would be done. Fin beat me to it.

"We got it," he whooped. "I wasn't even awake when she called. But then she called the home phone, and my mom woke me up and I was like, 'Joy who?'" He started laughing. "This is going to be hilarious! You can't be mad at me anymore. See, I knew you'd make it. You're just as good as Cassie Lott."

I laughed.

"We're going to make us some money, sweetcakes," he said. "I'm coming over so we can rehearse. I want to show you clips of Get Happy parties that I found on YouTube last night."

I stopped in the bathroom and smiled at myself again in the mirror.

This might actually be fun.

Downstairs, my mom was sitting at the computer in the kitchen with a huge mug of coffee in one hand, scrolling through her Facebook posts.

"I got a job," I announced.

She didn't respond.

"I got a job, Mom," I repeated.

She looked up. "What?"

"I got a job at Get Happy, doing kids' birthday parties. I go for training on Saturday."

"What in the world are you talking about?"

"I went to an audition with Fin for a job and I made it. We both made it."

She turned to face me, finally listening. "Why didn't you tell me about this before?"

"I didn't know if I'd make it."

Her face squinched. "Get Happy?"

"Yes. Get Happy. You can look them up. Get Happy, Incorporated. It's a big company. They're opening a new branch."

Her fingernails began clacking on the keyboard. She was silent as she searched through the site, clicking on the various pictures, lingering on one with a girl in a princess costume, singing in front of an obviously staged living room full of smiling children. "I don't know about this, Minny. The idea of going into strange people's houses . . ."

"I knew you'd say something like that. It's not strange people, Mom."

"What if it's a pervert's house?"

I laughed. "It's going to be a five-year-old's house, Mom. I don't think there are many five-year-old perverts."

"It could be a pervert pretending to have a five-year-old."

I gave her a kiss on the cheek and did a little waltz around the kitchen. "Mom, go back to Facebook and don't worry so much."

She smiled. "It's my job to keep you safe."

"I'll be safe. You should be happy I have a job, Mom."

"I'm pretty darn sure I could get you a job at the mall."

I hugged her. "This is a job *singing*."

"I just want to make sure this is legitimate. You have to be careful these days."

"It's not a scam. It's a national thing." I grabbed a

banana from the counter. "By the way, Fin is coming. We have to go over our scripts."

"I'm going to read up on this Get Happy thing. Did you clean your room?"

"Yes, Mommy." Calling her mommy usually put her in a good mood for some reason.

"Did you do a thorough job?"

"Thorough enough for me."

"Thorough enough for me?"

"You don't have to sleep there."

"Honey, if I go up there and discover that you didn't do a good job . . ."

"I'm going. I'm going."

~

I DECIDED THEN and there to stop thinking about the whole Keanu Choy thing. I didn't have to prove who he was, because I knew I didn't want to have anything to do with him. It didn't matter if he was a hotshot scientist or a convict. Either way, he'd left us high and dry, and if he thought one little necklace was going to make me forgive and forget, he could just jump off his boat and get eaten by sharks. I had a job and I was going to earn money. I was going to buy myself a uke and live happily ever after.

Fin came over, and we made hot chocolate and watched Get Happy videos on YouTube and read through our scripts like good little employees. The whole Get Happy enterprise was extremely corny, but it felt liberating to have something positive to focus on.

I stood up and said in my new, giddy Get Happy voice: "Let's be the best singing mermaid and pirate Joy Banks has ever seen. Let's make Joy Banks so excited she barfs."

Some people hear other people's words as conversation. Fin hears other people's words as cues. He immediately launched into singing the Get Happy song. I joined in, and we sang and danced around my room like insane asylum inmates. Thankfully, Joy Banks was not there to witness it, because if she had, she probably would have fired us. With a smile, of course.

~

> *Don't send me pearls or shiny things,*
> *Don't give me any bling.*
> *I'm not a girl who likes the tangled strings*
> > *of debt.*
> *Don't give me gifts so I'll forget*
> *Mistakes you made, you'll lose that bet.*
> *My heart's an iron fist inside my chest.*

Been giving it, giving it, giving it thought. . . .
I will not be bought.

I got tens and Benjamins,
Got 'em from the ATM.
Money makes the world go round.
Gotta have that ching, ching sound.

If our roads should intersect,
Turn to the right, and I'll go left
Elect to swerve and let's avoid the wreck.
Don't think I'll behave the way
You want me to. Don't hold your breath.
You'll get depressed. I'm not some Juliet.

I'll buy dresses, feather beds,
A brand-new house of gingerbread.
I'll buy the dye and dye my hair bright red.
Cash my checks and buy some leather,
Velvet gloves for colder weather.
Buy some love for me and all my friends.

No, no, no, no,
I'm not gonna owe you,
Not gonna owe you,
Not gonna owe you, oh . . .

7

TRAINING DAY

MY MOM INSISTED on driving me and Fin to the Get Happy office. The sun was out and it was abnormally warm — I mean take-your-coat-off warm — and most of the snow had melted.

When we stopped to get Fin, his two little brothers were kicking the soccer ball around and his dad was outside, too, in his big green muddy boots, tossing small branches and twigs into a wheelbarrow. I rolled down my window.

"Hi, Pat. Hey, Min darlin'. Congrats on your first real job." He took off his gardening gloves and walked over to the car. I've always loved Finnegan's dad. He was born and raised in Ireland and still has an Irish accent and all these freckles and reddish-brown hair that sticks up. Meteors could be headed toward Illinois, and everybody would panic and run around screaming their heads off, except Fin's dad, who would continue to calmly and cheerfully pick up twigs.

Fin walked out, and his brothers kicked the ball at him. He roared them away and got in the car.

"Have fun!" Mr. O'Connor said.

My mom wanted to come in and meet Joy, but I said absolutely not. She had already called Joy to make sure it was legitimate. We started having a big fight in the car, and Fin tried to negotiate peace, which didn't help, and I finally opened the door. "We are getting out now, Mom. And if you come in, I will die."

The heavens parted and, lo and behold, she showed me infinite mercy by driving away without saying another word.

As we walked up to the front door, Hayes arrived on foot, a big smile on his face, and shook our hands again, which cracked us up. "Minerva Watson and Finnegan O'Connor, future entertainers of young children, a pleasure to see you again."

"Hayes Martinelli, giver of plakettes," I said, "a pleasure to see you, too." And then I felt self-conscious, wondering if it was pathetic that I remembered the stone and his improvisational word for it, but he just laughed.

When we walked into the Get Happy office, Joy stood up from her desk and applauded.

"Wow," Hayes whispered. "I feel so loved."

"She is a desperate woman," I whispered back.

Cassie walked in. "Finally some great weather!" She twirled around, her coat flying open, another short skirt with bare legs.

"Yay! Here's my princess!" Joy said. "We're going to go over your scripts, learn the Get Happy theme song, and practice the games that you'll each be leading. But, to put everybody in the Get Happy mood, first we're going to try on our costumes!" She wheeled out a rack with four large white garment bags and four white boxes.

"I was thinking of doing my hair up like this," Cassie said, and in one deft motion, she swept her long hair into an updo.

"Yes!" Joy said. "Perfect. These are high-quality costumes, so take good care of them. Your costume goes in the garment bag, your accessories go in your box. We meet here, change here, and then I take everybody in the van and do a drop-off and pickup." She pulled the first bag and box off the rack — Cassie's — and started going over it with her.

"Shoot me now," Hayes whispered.

"You're a cowboy," Fin said. "You can shoot yourself."

"I don't think that's the proper Get Happy attitude," I said.

"What's up with cowboys anyway? Why are kids supposed to want a cowboy party? What do cowboys even do?"

"They eat beans and sit around the campfire," Fin said. "And then they do it with the cows."

I laughed. "Get Happy is probably thinking more like Woody."

Fin started singing the theme song from *Toy Story* and then he said, "Golly, Hayes, everybody wants a cowboy friend because they're loyal and brave and true."

"Aw, shucks," Hayes said. "You're right."

"Darn tootin'," I added.

I was next. Joy handed over my garment bag and box. I lifted the lid off and pulled out a wig of long red hair. Fin pulled a wig of dreadlocks out of his box. We looked at each other and burst out laughing.

"Let's see yours," I said to Hayes.

He pulled out a cowboy hat and a fake gun. He pulled the gun's trigger, and a flag popped out, which said HAPPY BIRTHDAY.

Joy snatched it. "Oh, rattlefinks! I meant to put that away. We had complaints, so we can't use it anymore."

Fin glanced at me, loving "rattlefinks," and trying not to laugh out loud.

"I don't get a gun," Hayes said. "I don't get a wig. What kind of cowboy am I?"

I nudged my box toward him. "Wanna switch?"

He smiled. "I guess cowboy ain't so bad."

Dimples aren't fair. They make it very hard to focus.

"Try on your costumes and let me know if anything needs adjusting." Joy gestured to the back. Curtains suspended from rods separated the back of the room into two changing areas. "Hayes, you can wear your own jeans with your outfit."

Cassie and I took our costumes into our area. *This is going to be fun*, I told myself. *Just have fun.*

With serious difficulty and mounting horror, I pulled on the tan bodysuit, positioned the stiff, seashell-shaped pink cups, and then struggled into a tight green tube skirt with iridescent chiffon flounces at the bottom — the fins of a mermaid tail.

"That is so pretty," Cassie lied through her perfect teeth. "I wish I got the mermaid."

I looked at myself in the mirror. My hips and thighs looked enormous.

"Help me with mine." She turned so I could zip up her white satin princess dress. "It fits." She spun around in front of the mirror and then she went out to show Joy.

Fin's voice came from the other side of the curtain. "These pants make my butt look HUGE. I want to wear my own jeans, like Hayes."

"No," Joy called out.

"Can I skip the wig and wear my own hair?" I called. "No."

"This is a disaster," I whispered to Fin through the curtain. "I hate you for getting me involved with this." I put on my long red wig and tiara, picked up the glittering pink trident.

"Rattlefinks, I need eyeliner," Fin said, and then started laughing.

"Boys do not wear eyeliner," Joy called out.

I braced for the side view. "This is truly hideous. Fin . . ."

"Seriously. I need eyeliner," he whispered through the curtain. "And a tan."

"I need a tan, too," I said. "I look like a corpse."

"We need to buy some of that fake tan-in-a-tube stuff. Wait. I think I put the shirt on backward."

Hayes's voice came through: "These buttonholes are too small for the buttons. How do cowboys live this like?"

I turned to see how the tail looked from the back. "Joy, can I be something different?" I asked through the curtain. "This costume doesn't fit."

"Absolutely not."

"You *have* to be a mermaid, Minerva," Fin said, and did the evil witch laugh from the *Little Mermaid* movie. "Remember how we decided that our utility closet was Ursula's true lair and that her evil minions lived in the water heater?"

"We didn't decide that," I said. "You told me that, and you were completely convincing. I was terrified. I've been terrified of utility closets ever since."

Hayes's voice: "I look ridiculous."

Fin: "I want those boots. You are so lucky. Trade."

Hayes: "Dude, the wig is hilarious."

Joy: "Come out!"

Cassie, Fin, and Hayes were all together, laughing. I peeked out. Cassie linked arms with Hayes and Fin and started singing the Get Happy song. She looked amazing. They looked funny, but really cute. Fin's pants were too long and the dreadlock wig was crooked, but he was rocking the frilly white pirate shirt and the vest. Hayes, lean and taller, looked uncomfortably adorable, like a cowboy who woke up and found himself in somebody else's dream, with boots a little too big and hat a little too small.

"Get out here, Minerva," Fin cried.

I could have dissolved into a puddle of self-loathing or taken off the costume and quit on the spot, but the less embarrassing thing was to play the clown. I put on a fake smile and walked out singing "Under the Sea."

Fin howled and hugged me, crushing my pink shell cups. "Ariel."

I bowed and my tiara fell off, which gave me something to do while Joy took a million photos of Cassie.

When she took one of Fin, he said, "Arrrrrgh," and

tried to pull his fake sword from his scabbard, but it got stuck and he swore.

"For heaven's sake, don't say that, Finnegan," Joy said. "Say 'fudderudder.'"

"Fudderudder!" Fin screamed, and the way he said it cheered me up for a moment and almost made me pee in my mermaid suit.

8

JEALOUSY REARS ITS UGLY HEAD

I WAS IN A VIM-and-vigory mood, getting ready for our first gigs, practicing my mermaid lines, and playing the Get Happy theme song on my fake cookie-tin uke in front of the mirror in my bedroom. I had the brilliant idea that, once I bought a real uke, I could play it for all the little kiddies at future birthday parties.

After school one day, I got up the nerve to return to Tenley's Music Store to test-drive my new Get Happy material on the uke of my dreams.

If you love ukes, entering a music store and seeing a row of them hanging up is like swimming into a cave and discovering a hoard of treasures.

The guy behind the counter — the one with the disgusting chest-length beard — gave me this look when I walked in because I had been there so many times before. "Let me guess," he said. "You're in the market for an uke?"

That *an* was not a typo, by the way. He pronounces it *oo*-kulele, not *you*-kulele. He told me once in his usual condescending manner that it can be pronounced either way, but that true aficionados prefer *oo*-kulele. I appreciate vocabulary. I do not appreciate condescension.

"I have birthday money," I told him. "I've narrowed it down to two models and I just need to play those to decide."

He shot me a poisonous look and said: "You know which one you want. *I* know which one you want. This isn't a practice studio. This is a store."

"Please?" I stood for a moment, lurking in the doorway, drooling over the ukes. I'll do anything, sir; I'll trade my soul for one moment of happiness. Please?

He stepped from behind the counter, hoisting up his baggy jeans. "This is the last time." He lifted the one I wanted off the hook and gave it to me with his hairy arms and then went back to his magazine.

Gratefully, I sat on an amp and played through the chord shapes that I had learned from the book Fin gave me. The uke just felt right in my arms. I'm little. It's little. I pluck it, without really even knowing what I'm doing, and it sounds beautiful. Other instruments aren't like that. Blow into a clarinet without knowing what you're doing and it sounds like a dying seagull.

When another guy came in to actually buy something, I put the uke back and slipped out. For a while, I wandered around downtown Evanston, imagining a whole scenario in which I stroll into Tenley's with my first paycheck and shock the mice right out of the guy's beard by buying my uke. I would bring it to Get Happy parties and wow the children and parents by singing my own songs—clever and funny and impressive songs. Minerva the Mermaid would become the most popular children's party entertainer in the northwest suburbs of Chicago, more popular, even than, say, the princess, because I would have some original talent to share. I love daydreams.

As I wandered, I also looked at stuff in shop windows, but really I was looking at my reflection, imagining how much better I would look if I had a uke sticking out of my backpack. I wanted people to see me and think, *That girl is a songwriter.* Maybe that seems shallow, but to be good at something, you have to first look the part.

~

SOMEWHERE IN the bottom of my brain, I remembered Cassie Lott saying that she was writing a blog about diving. I should have left that alone, because, really, in the big picture of my life, Cassie Lott should have meant nothing to me, but the murky undertow inside me was hoping that if I looked at it, I would discover she had a flaw — perhaps her writing would reveal a decidedly inferior vocabulary, for example — and I could hold her flaw up to the light and feel better about myself. A more highly evolved person would not have such a thought, and I am embarrassed to admit it. But at least I am being honest.

When I had a moment alone at home, I did a little search.

Seeing the Sea through My Eyes —
a blog by Cassie Lott

The blog was about scuba diving, not swim-team diving. When she had said her hobby was diving, I had erroneously pictured her on a diving board. Photoshopped into the background of her blog was her official scuba-diving certification card. The portrait on the right showed her on a beach in a short-sleeved wet suit, with her long wet hair pulled back by the face mask on her head. Her arms were muscular yet feminine, her abdomen as flat and hard as a surfboard.

My face burned. Instead of finding a flaw in her, I now had scuba-diving prowess thrown in my face. How lovely.

Each blog entry was a photo of something she saw on this trip to Cozumel or that trip to Costa Rica — like a shell or a jellyfish or whale tails — with an explanation of why it was so beautiful.

Winter Break. Sunset on the Pacific Ocean.

Two humpback whales break the surface and submerge in a paired arc. I loved capturing this moment. Their bodies are as graceful as ballet dancers, the flap of their flukes against the orange sky like their final jeté before disappearing offstage.

As if anybody needs your little metaphor, Cassie. Let nature speak for itself.

9

THE FIRST GIG

FIN AND I SPLIT the cost of overnight bronze self-tanning lotion and slathered it on each other's faces the night before the big day.

I enjoyed a restful slumber and then I woke up to a horrible smell. My first thought: A cancerous rodent had crawled under my bed and died. Panicky, I got up and looked around and then realized the aroma was coming from my own hand. My palm was streaked with a brownish-orange color and smelled like death.

I ran to the mirror. My face looked like a decomposing pumpkin. I called Fin.

"Are you mad at me?" he asked, his voice racked

with anguish. "I already tried washing it. Seven times. It's not coming off."

"Do you smell like a corpse?"

"Yes! What is up with that?" he screamed.

"We can't go," I said.

"Yes, we can. It's not so bad," he said. "Once we have our wigs and costumes on, we'll look fine."

And so . . . off we went to Get Happy headquarters with radically unnatural complexions. When Joy saw us walk through the door, she dropped the box she was holding. "Son of a biscuit, what happened to your faces?"

Fin and I looked at each other. Son of a biscuit. If the universe couldn't give us nicely tanned skin, at least it gave us Joy's fake profanity.

Cassie and Hayes were already there.

Cassie laughed and then said, "Sorry."

I didn't know how Hayes was reacting because I was too embarrassed to look at him.

"We look like oompa loompas, don't we?" Fin laughed and started singing the oompa loompa song.

"This isn't funny!" Joy cried, and glared at us.

We put on our costumes and hustled into the van just as it started to lightly snow.

Hayes's party was first. When the van stopped and Hayes got out, Joy yelped, "Leave your coat in here! Your characters do not wear coats!"

As Hayes threw his coat back in the car, Cassie hopped out. She gave him a hug and straightened his bolo tie. "Break a leg, Hayes."

"She is so sweet," Joy said.

My house was next. When we pulled up, a mom waved from the doorway. "The girls are all so excited," she called. Fat snowflakes were coming down. She opened an umbrella and came out to meet us. I jumped down from the van and she looked at my face. "Oh."

That's what she said. *Oh.*

"Get under that umbrella, Minerva, so you don't get your costume wet," Joy said.

"I'm a mermaid fresh from the sea," I said. "I absolutely adore precipitation."

Joy shot me a look. She wasn't sure if I was being facetious or getting into character.

The mom led me into one of those big family rooms that rich people have, facing the back of the house. A table was piled high with gifts. Ten girls were watching some tweeny-bopper, boy-band concert movie on the largest screen in the Western Hemisphere.

"Look who's here!" The mom turned off the TV, and the room erupted in protests.

"Wait . . . the best part is coming," one of the girls said.

"But it's time for the big surprise." The mom held out her hands toward me, still standing in the doorway. The girls turned and stared.

Silence.

The script I had spent all week memorizing was for four-year-olds. These girls looked like they wanted to cut me in pieces and throw me into piranha-infested waters.

Even though I knew it was ridiculous, the script was all I had, so I smiled and said my first few lines. "Hi. I've been swimming around all morning searching for a birthday girl to see. I know there's one here. . . . Who could it be?"

Dead silence.

"Here she is," the mom said. "It's Samantha!" She tried to pull her daughter to her feet.

One girl said to another, "Why is her face orange?"

I wanted to turn and make a run for it.

"Hold on. I have to record this." The dad walked

in, holding his cell phone up, video rolling. "Look, it's Ursula!"

"Ariel," the mom corrected him.

"Hi, Samantha," I said. "Happy birthday."

The girl whispered something to her mom.

"No, not yet," the mother whispered. "We can turn it back on later. This is going to be fun."

"Wow!" the dad said. "A real mermaid! Why did the mermaid cross the road?"

Cavernous silence.

"To get to the other tide!" The dad laughed. "Are you from the Atlantic Ocean or the Pacific Ocean, Miss Mermaid?"

Not knowing what else to do, I kept going with the script. "How many of you know the Get Happy song?"

No hands.

"It's easy. I'll sing and you can join in. I have some instruments. . . ."

"Oooh, instruments!" the dad said.

There's this fake voice that grown-ups use with kids that should be against the law. Gosh, kids, isn't this fun? The answer is no. People who use this voice should be locked up. Samantha's parents were world-class fakers, and I was committing the crime right along with them.

I passed out the plastic maracas and sang through the song and announced the game.

"Mom," Samantha whispered again into her mother's ear. The girl's face was turning a brighter shade of red every second.

"Just start the game," the dad said. "I'm sure Sammy will join in. Sammy, your mom went to a lot of trouble for this."

"John, that is not the point," the mom snapped.

I was supposed to do this whole intro to the game, but I set out the props and cut straight to the rules. "So you get a starfish and you try to throw it into the empty bucket. If you get one in, you'll get a prize."

"What do we get?" a girl asked.

The prize — a cheap necklace of fake beads — wasn't going to win them over, so I told them that I'd hand out the prizes after everybody played.

"This will be fun. Who wants to go first?" the mom asked.

Amazingly, a round-faced girl closest to me raised her hand. I wanted to hug her. I wanted to take her home with me. I wanted to hire that tweeny-bopper boy band to lift her up in their arms and sing a pop song about her.

One by one, each girl stood up and played the game, Samantha last. The girls took the gold, silver, and green necklaces from me as if they were strands of rotten sea kelp.

"Put them on! We'll take a picture. We'll post it on Facebook so all your cousins can see it."

The girls put on the rotten kelp, and the mom made them gather around me.

"Smile and say, *'Mermaid'*!" the dad said.

I imagined how my orange face was going to look, captured for all time, and posted online.

"Mermaid," I said.

Snap.

~

"So . . . how was it, Minerva?" Joy asked.

Hayes was already in the van. He tipped his cowboy hat and said, "Howdy," in an adorable way.

"It was great," I said, and then mouthed the word *terrible* to Hayes as I passed him on my way to the backseat.

"Well, that's good," Joy said.

Hayes smiled. "Mine was actually okay."

"Two for two," Joy said.

My mom had left seven messages on my phone, asking how the first gig went. I texted back: **Great.**

Cassie was next.

The temperature had warmed up, and none of the snow had stuck. As Joy pulled up to the house, the sun burst through the clouds.

"Hallelujah," Joy said, turning off the engine. She glanced at her watch. "She should be done any minute."

My stomach growled and I was seriously considering asking Joy if she might have packed any snacks for a hardworking mermaid, when the front door of the house opened and Cassie floated out, surrounded by five-year-olds. The mother tried to get the girls back into the house, but they followed without their coats on.

"It's okay," Cassie said to the mom. "We'll have one last good-bye." Quickly, she lined up the girls and waltzed down the line, giving each child a hug and a tap on the head with her wand.

"Thank the Lord." Joy sighed. "Look at that. She's a natural."

Cassie daintily pulled up her gown, ran to the van, turned, blew kisses, and got inside.

"Wait!" The dad came running out the front door with a pink cupcake and a ten-dollar bill and handed them through the window to Cassie before waving good-bye.

Joy was beaming. "They loved you."

Cassie handed the tip to Joy.

"No. Tips are yours to keep."

Cassie smiled. "I can't believe I'm getting paid to do this." She turned to Hayes and me, her face glowing. "Isn't it great?"

"Yep," I said. "It's a barrel of monkeys."

She broke off a piece of cupcake and put it between her ruby lips. "Yum. Want a bite, anyone?"

I was dying for a bite, but I shook my head and lied: "I had, like, ten pieces of cake at Samantha's house."

Hayes took a bite. Cassie chattered away, filling us in on all the details of the amazing job she did, and filling up the car with the sugary smell of frosting. Finally, we picked up Fin.

Just seeing his orange face and funny fake dreadlocks as he climbed into the van cheered me up.

"Children are savages," he said. "That was the most exhausting thing I've ever done in my life. CUPCAKE?" He looked at Cassie. "I didn't get anything."

"Here." Cassie handed him her last bite.

"How did it go?" I asked as he stuffed it into his mouth.

"They were horrible. They laughed at my song. So I ditched the script and made them walk the plank."

Joy's head snapped around. "YOU WHAT?"

"I picked the two beastliest boys to be crocodiles and told them to lie down. Then, one by one, I made the others jump off the chair, and when they landed on the floor, the crocodiles got to bite their little ankles. They loved it."

"Son of a freaking biscuit! Do not go off script," Joy said. "Somebody could get hurt."

We both started to lose it.

"Whatever you're laughing at back there, it's not funny," Joy said.

10

THE BLOG

CASSIE LOTT'S BLOG was like a Dead-Sea-salt-induced itch that I had to scratch. I was simply curious, I told myself. Just a bit of harmless, mildly jealous snooping.

Subscribe! Follow me on Twitter!
Follow me on Facebook!

She had 2,433 followers and was following 1,112 people and organizations.

She hadn't posted anything new — perhaps she was too busy with her volunteer work or all her extracurricular activities, I thought — so I resorted to looking at previous entries, when a photo she had posted in August jumped out to bite me in the jugular: a seahorse.

A Glimpse in the Wild

Whenever I dive, I keep a close lookout
for seahorses to photograph for the SOS
(Save Our Seahorse) survey project, which
is collecting data to document the lives of
seahorses, but most are tiny and shy and hard
to find. I got lucky today and spotted this
Pacific seahorse off the coast of Monterey.
The Pacific seahorse is the largest species.
This one is about five inches.

See how its tail is wrapped around the
blade of sea grass? This is called a *holdfast*.
After a seahorse is a week or two old, it finds
something to cling to so that it isn't swept
away by a current. Beautiful, isn't it?

The entry had seven comments. I should have turned off the computer. I should have listened to that inner voice that said: *You don't need to see more.* Instead, I scrolled down and saw it.

Keanu Choy says:

I stood up and literally yelped — I could because my mom wasn't home. Then I looked at the screen again.

Keanu Choy says:
Congrats! Yes, the holdfast is critical. I'm sure this blog will inspire other young divers to join in the Save Our Seahorse Project! Thanks, Cassie!

After calming down, I reasoned that, as weird as it felt, this actually wasn't weird at all. It made sense. Cassie's profile said she was volunteering at the Shedd Aquarium, and she was following both the Shedd Aquarium and the SOS Project on Twitter. I clicked a link to the SOS Project, and it was all about encouraging "recreational divers" to document seahorses. Her name was on a long list of "Seahorse Spotters."

I don't know why I was surprised. Seahorses live in the sea, and they are very compelling little creatures, and lots of scuba divers must be interested in playing hide-and-seek with them. Keanu Choy probably commented on the blogs of all his followers who posted pictures of seahorses. They were cyber save-the-seahorse buddies. How cute. How educational. How adorably nauseating.

He had shared six of Cassie's blog entries with his own followers and had left several comments on other entries.

Keanu Choy says:
I agree. The sea slug is beautiful!

Keanu Choy says:
This is a gorgeous description of sea dragons, Cassie!

Keanu Choy says:
I love the way you captured that moment when the sun came shining onto the reef. Well done!

On and on. The man loves his exclamation points!

I stared at the screen. I got up and paced. Then I sat down and created a new email account. Name? Landlover@yahoo.com.

Back on Cassie's blog.

Would you like to leave a comment?

Yes, I would.

Landlover says:

This blog is extremely uninformative. The writer obviously just loves the sound of her own voice.

Send.

I imagined how excited Cassie would be to see a comment from a new visitor and then how hurt she'd be to read it. Within seconds, though, I felt sick to my stomach. That's the thing about being mean: You have this rush, this wicked thrill, but then it fades quickly and you're left feeling like scum.

I texted Fin. He didn't answer, and I remembered that he was at a cousin's wedding or funeral in Mundelein. I have learned from experience that Irish people have way too many relatives. I wasn't about to tell him that Keanu Choy commented on Cassie Lott's blog, because he would tell me to immediately find out if he was my dad and I wasn't ready for that, but I needed to hear Fin's voice. Even if it was just in a text. I sent him three more messages.

Finally, he replied: What's up in Minervaland?
Me: I'm leaving evil comments on Cassie's blog.
Fin: I want to see them!!!!!

Me: She irritates me.

Fin: Perfect people are perfectly irritating.

Me: Don't do any more Soul to Sole workshops with her. I forbid it.

Fin: I told you I'm not going back there. The studio smells like horse manure. The teacher doesn't use proper hygiene products. Chow time. Guess what the bread basket has in it?

Me: Bread.

Fin: Biscuits!!!!!!!!

Me: Son of a biscuit.

Fin: Nummy nummy.

Me: Why doesn't anybody say daughter of a biscuit?

Fin: Too many syllabyllables.

11

THE SQUID
& THE PROMISE

NOTE: OVERNIGHT self-tanning lotion takes days to fade. Rick Rogan, the mean guy in my first-period class, had so much fun with me that week, he should have paid me.

Excited to have a job, I blocked him out. Nothing like walking down the hallway of high school knowing you are employed. The pukey green paint on the walls seems less nauseating, the dribble of lukewarm water coming from the water fountain seems less contaminated, the babble of voices cascading down the hallway seems less damaging to the brain.

During my classes, my teachers contributed to my well-being by doing lots of PowerPoints. Everybody knows that as soon as the lights go off and the projector turns on, nobody pays attention. I love a dark classroom and the drone of a teacher's voice. I spent the week hunched over my songwriting journal cleverly disguised as an academic notebook, letting new song ideas spring forth and looking up every now and then to make it seem as if I were engrossed in the properties of quadratic equations or the endoplasmic reticulum of cells.

On Friday of that week, Hayes Martinelli texted during school, asking if Fin and I had any interest in taking the El into Chicago and hanging out downtown with him.

I ducked into the doorway of an empty classroom to avoid the passing stampede and stared at the text for so long my phone actually went black.

I was about to call Finnegan when he beat me to it. Hayes had texted both of us.

"Do you think he invited Cassie?" I asked. "I mean, is this like a Get Happy bonding thing?"

"I don't know," Fin said.

"Find out."

"You find out."

I texted Hayes back. **Cool idea. Is Cassie coming?**

His answer: **No. She said she has a dance class.**

A maddening answer. I would have much preferred: *No. I didn't invite her.* But I actually agreed to go and we both texted yes to Hayes.

I would have gone and had a great time, but then the universe served up the squid.

In bio, we were ending the semester with a unit on dissection, and that afternoon, we were greeted by the pungent smell of formaldehyde, and trays on our tables bearing dead brown squids. Immediate hysterical gagging and laughing all around. I was fine with it at first. I had no problem slicing into the flesh with a razor-sharp scalpel, pinning open the creature, and locating the heart, stomach, intestines, ink sac, and other miscellaneous organs.

But then while we were washing up, Ms. Feinstein walked over to her computer and projected the Shedd Aquarium Web site on the SmartScreen and gushed about their free lecture series and showed us the Shedd's schedule of events. There it was: Keanu Choy, winner of the Loire Award for Marine Research, was giving a talk in conjunction with a special seahorse exhibit on Saturday, April 15.

My teacher went on to show us her own photos that she'd taken scuba diving in Florida over winter break. Several other people jumped in with tales of their scuba experiences, and I felt as if I'd been sucked into the Bermuda Triangle. Suddenly, everyone in Illinois was into scuba diving. It made me want to eject my lunch from the anterior cavity, otherwise known as my stomach.

Ms. Feinstein caught me on the way out. "Sometimes, kids get hit after they're all done dissecting," she said, obviously thinking my distress was due to being grossed out by the squid. "Splash some water on your face and you'll be fine."

That's how life works. You don't hear much about scuba diving until you don't *want* to hear about scuba diving and then it's everywhere.

As soon as we were dismissed for the day, I sat on the bench outside the school's front entrance and called Fin. It was cold again; even though the sun was shining, the bench was a giant ice cube. He answered on the third buzz.

"Fin, I can't go to Chicago."

"You have to. Hayes is meeting me at my locker and we're going to come find you. Where are you?"

"I can't go. Feinstein mentioned Keanu Choy in class and the whole thing made me sick."

"What did she say?"

"He's doing a free lecture, and the Shedd is so wonderful, and everything is beautiful under the sea, blah, blah, blee. I'm holding down my vomit."

Background voices and locker slams were all I heard in the phone.

"Fin, did you hear what I just said?"

His breath came out in a sigh. "You are perseverating on this Keanu Choy connection, which might be a total fiction, Minerva. You need to go ask your mom right now."

"I knew you'd say that."

"Because it makes sense."

"I can't — "

"If you don't, I'm going to find a new best friend," he said.

"Don't be mean."

"I'm not being mean, I'm exhibiting tough love." More locker noises and then his voice: "You have two choices. Go home now and ask her. Or come with us, have fun, and then talk to her as soon as you get home."

"I can't do either of those."

A pause. Then he asked, "Do you want me to tell Hayes I can't go?"

I sat there, staring at the dead grass under the big, bare tree, my fingers freezing. I didn't want to be that girl, the one who is so needy she prevents her best friend from having fun. "Go," I said. "Tell Hayes I got sick."

"You sure you don't want to come?"

"Yeah — " My voice caught on itself. "Fin?"

"Yeah?"

"If you dump me, I'm going to shrivel up and die."

I could hear his eyes smile. "I'm not dumping you for anybody, sweetcakes," he said. *I will always love Minerva. I would follow her to Persia,"* he sang in the most heart-melting, lullaby voice.

"Promise?"

"Promise."

12

AUNT JOAN
& THE TRUTH

IN CASE YOU didn't know, giving your best friend your blessing to frolic with a new, nicely dimpled friend while you are wrestling with fear makes for an excruciating evening. That day, I rushed to the music store after school, hoping the bearded guy wouldn't be there so I could play my uke, which would have calmed me down. No such luck. I walked home. Slowly. When my mom arrived from work, I tried and failed to think of a way to bring up the subject. After dinner, I sat on the couch in the living room, feigning interest in a movie, while she began her seasonal redecorating campaign.

As she was putting away winter-themed knickknacks and setting out valentine-themed ones, she found Aunt Joan's birthday card behind an end table and held it up. "Did you send Aunt Joan a thank-you letter?"

The no that was all over my face was the least of my worries.

She stopped and looked at me. "That is not the right attitude, Minny. I was going to call her tonight, and now I'll be embarrassed. It's already the beginning of February. You've had plenty of time."

I was about to say something when a window opened in my mind, allowing a new thought to fly in: Aunt Joan would know about Keanu Choy. The realization was obvious and big and strangely shocking. It was as if an ostrich had flown into the room. Unaware, my mom went on with her lecture about courtesy and gratitude while she set a trio of fat red candles and a garland of foil hearts on the coffee table and hung up a red wooden sign saying: LOVE IS HOME.

Keeping my eyes on the television and my voice under control, I promised to write a thank-you.

After a few more minutes of decorating, she took the tub of valentine decorations upstairs, and when I heard the low murmuring of her voice, I knew she was on the phone.

I walked upstairs. She was in the bathroom, phone in one hand, replacing the white star-shaped Christmas soaps in the dish with red heart-shaped ones.

"Mom," I whispered. "Is that Aunt Joan? I want to say thanks."

She mouthed: *That is so nice,* and then she said, "Hold on, Joan; Minerva wants to say hi."

I took the phone. "Hi, Aunt Joan. Thanks for the dough. Sorry I didn't send a thank-you."

"Hi, Minerva," my aunt said. "Good to hear your voice. You sound older, girl!" Her voice always surprised me because it sounded like my mom's and altogether different from my mom's at the same time. "You got snow?"

"Did. Not now."

"Snowing here like there's no tomorrow."

While she began telling me a story about their truck getting stuck — she always had a story — I gave my mom one of those looks like *You know Aunt Joan, this is going to be a while,* and I made a sign-language gesture that I was going to get something to drink. Then I nonchalantly headed downstairs with the phone while my mom kept decorating.

I laughed about the truck story until I got to the kitchen, which was far enough away for some sonic privacy, and then I said: "Hey. I have to do this genealogy report for school. You know, on immigration and everything. I was just wondering . . . about my dad. . . . Is he Hawaiian or Japanese or what?" I took a breath and tried to sound casual. "I mean, with a name like Keanu Choy, I wasn't sure."

There was a split second of hesitation. "Is — is your mom finally talking about this, Minerva? She had a no-talking policy about Keanu for years."

The sound of his name coming out of my aunt's mouth sucked all the oxygen out of the room.

"Yeah." I tried to laugh. "We've talked. It's just not her favorite subject." I opened the sliding glass door in our kitchen, stepped onto our dark, cold deck for air, and closed the door behind me.

"That's the understatement of the year," she said. "Listen, I never really hit it off with Keanu. He was a real go-getter and had a high opinion of himself, if you know what I mean, but that's not a crime."

"Yeah. My mom told me everything, but I just forgot if she said he was from Hawaii or what," I said. The trick was to keep the conversation going.

"Hawaii. He had relatives in California," she said. "So when he got that job offer out there, I knew it was over. I thought your mom should try to at least work out the custody with him, but she wouldn't budge, and he wouldn't budge. And when that whole Disneyland thing happened . . . I think that was a clincher."

"Yeah," I said carefully, facing the house so I could see if my mom was coming. "My mom said Disneyland was a clincher. . . ."

Aunt Joan sighed. "Do you remember that? You were so little."

"I remember bits and pieces," I said.

"I'll never forget that call from your mom . . . and the tears. . . ."

"Yeah," I said as if I knew the whole story. "She was really upset."

"I was in Chicago then, do you remember? You were so cute on the way to the airport, so excited about going. Your mom was pretty darn sure that once he saw the two of you again, he'd come back."

"So Disneyland was her idea. I always wondered why we went there. We never did any other big trips except to see you."

"No. She said Disneyland was his idea. And then you guys get all the way out there and . . . how could he not show up? Who would do that to a wife and a three-year-old daughter? Just not show up? Not pay for it? Say, oh, I changed my mind. And don't get me started on child support. I've been telling her she should sue his pants off. He's got the dough."

The deck seemed to be tipping. "I know, but my mom has wanted nothing to do with him."

"You got that right. When she told me about the new wife and stepdaughter, I knew that was the last straw for her. Evidently, he's got the money to support them."

All the blood rushed from my head. I had the strange feeling that I was falling, but I was still standing.

Wife and stepdaughter.

"Listen, that school project sounds like a bunch of bull honkey," Aunt Joan went on. "Just write in whatever you want and don't worry about it. I know I'm not supposed to say this kind of thing, but ninety-nine percent of what you have to do in high school is a complete waste of time."

I tried to laugh it off, and began to shiver, shoeless out there on the deck, my thin socks useless, suddenly overcome by the cold.

"Look. Your mom and I are very different, but we're both Watsons. We like to talk, but we don't go deep. You know what I mean. But if this stuff is really on your mind, you should try to talk about it with her. I know it's hard, but you should try."

Through the glass door, I saw my mom walk into the kitchen. She noticed me and gave me this look like, *Who talks on the phone outside in winter?*

"Yeah," I said quickly. "It's not a big deal. It just came up because of the genealogy thing. Like you said, it's a waste of time."

"Hey, when are you coming to the ranch again for a visit?"

My mom opened the door.

"I don't know. I'll ask." I smiled at my mom. "Aunt Joan wants to know when we're coming out for a visit."

My mom rolled her eyes.

"Tell that mom of yours to get both your butts out here this summer."

"Okay, Aunt Joan."

My mom took the phone and resumed her conversation with Aunt Joan, pulling me inside. I was worried that Aunt Joan would tell her what we were talking about, but my mom launched into a whole thing about a recipe, and the conversation ended normally.

While I was in a daze of epic proportions, I made up a story about how Fin and I had a project to work on and how we were meeting downtown and, no, I didn't need a ride, and I grabbed my coat and walked out the door. At the end of the block, I called him. He and Hayes were just getting off the train — they had stayed downtown to eat — and he could tell by the sound of my voice that I was in trouble, and he said he could meet me at the Pan Asia Café to talk.

"Alone, please," I said. "And don't tell Hayes that there's anything wrong. And please don't tell me anything about the fun you had."

Fin had no money left and I had a total of two dollars in my pocket, so I ordered a Coke, and the waitress gave us an annoyed look.

As soon as she was gone, I let it out. "My dad is Keanu Choy. He isn't a drug dealer or a convict. He's a hotshot Hawaiian scientist with a high opinion of himself." I went on to explain about the phone call with Aunt Joan.

"So he met your mom when he was an intern at the Shedd Aquarium?" Fin asked.

"Then he left us, moved to California for a job, and never looked back because he's a go-getter. A guy who goes to get stuff. A guy who goes to get ahead."

"Then he moved back here?"

"The aquarium offered him a big kahuna job and he couldn't pass it up, being the go-getter that he is, and by then he had found himself a lovely new family."

"You're kidding?"

"A wife and stepdaughter."

"Son of an unbelievable biscuit."

"Yep. He is here now, with them."

"What are you going to do?"

My anger was turning into exhaustion. "First, I need to forget about him and move on with my life. Second, I have to quit Get Happy."

"Why?"

"Because Cassie reminds me of him."

"What does Cassie have to do with it?"

"She is a recreational scuba diver and member of his SOS club."

"What?"

"I didn't tell you before, but I found out on her blog. They're Save Our Seahorse buddies. They're saving the world one seahorse at a time. He encourages her and all his followers by posting positive comments on their sites with lots of exclamation points!"

"You are freaking kidding me."

"No. Every time I see Cassie, I'll be reminded of him. I need to move on with my life. I think my mom is right. He isn't worth the time of day. I'm just going to forget about him. I don't want to talk about it and I don't want you to pressure me into contacting him."

"On one condition."

"What?"

"You can't quit Get Happy."

"I have to."

"If you quit, it will mean that you're missing out on something good because of him. It's like giving him the time of day." He squeezed my hand. "Think of *me*. I would be missing out on fun with you because of him. *And* you're going to buy your uke with the first paycheck." He raised his eyebrows.

"But Cassie will induce projectile vomiting."

"Pretend she isn't there," he said. "You don't have to spend time with her. Just the rides to and from the gigs. Who cares if she's buddy-buddy with the seahorse people?" He slid the Coke in front of me. "Come on, Min. Drink from the river of life. Drink from the cup of vigor and vim. Do not let this guy rain on your parade. Do not let this guy ruin your life."

I had to smile.

The waitress came and asked us again if we wanted anything.

When she left, Fin admitted that he had looked up Keanu Choy after I first told him of my suspicions. "There is one positive here," he said. "At least you know you have good genes."

"They're not good genes," I said.

"He's gorgeous and smart and successful. They're good genes."

"They're mean genes."

He crushed a napkin into a ball and threw it at me. "Min, you don't have mean genes."

"I have a couple."

"We all have a couple. Except maybe Joy Banks. She has gosh-darn sweetie-pie genes."

I felt tears coming on and didn't want to cry, so I started to swear. Fin lunged across the table to give me a hug and said, "Say, 'fudderudder'!"

I laughed and swallowed back my tears and then I took a big gulp from the cup of vigor and vim.

13

EMBRACING
MY NEW LIFE

I HAD A FLURRY of songwriting, filling page after page in my songwriting journal. Twice after school, I went to Tenley's Music Store and got to play my new songs on a real uke because the bearded guy wasn't there. On the third day, he rose from the dead and was sitting behind the counter when I walked in. Needless to say, I turned around and hightailed it out of there.

Thank goodness for cookie-tin ukes. At least I had something to hold. In the privacy of my room, I strummed air and sang my heart out.

SALT

I am the salt
In the water,
A far cry from sweet.
I am the salt,
And it's all your fault.
I am the salt in the sea.

You got a boat.
Think you own the sea.
Want to sail here
And say hello to me?
You're still a nobody.

Don't try to hold me. Oh, no.
Don't try to own me. Oh, no.
Don't you try to know me.

Waves throw castaways
On the sand:
Broken seashells
And rusted cans—
That's what you mean to me.

And I won't waste time
Thinking of you,
Won't chase the tide
Of that deep and bonny blue.

I am the salt
In the water,
A far cry from sweet.
I am the salt,
And it's all your fault.
I am the salt in the sea
In the sea.

14

BREAKTHROUGH GIG

As you know, time does not stop to allow you to ponder the flotsam and jetsam of your mind. When you're a working girl, you have to put on your wig and your tail and get to work, gosh darn it.

Fin was right. I could tune Cassie out. Another week flew by and it was time for another set of Get Happy parties. I was especially excited because after this one, we were getting our first paychecks.

The day began with a pep talk from Joy and helpful advice on how to guarantee a tip.

"Flirt with the parents!" Cassie chimed in.

"Cassie!" Joy exclaimed.

"Not gross flirting. Just things like, 'Wow, I love your window treatments.'"

Fin and Hayes laughed. "That's brilliant," Fin said.

We piled into the van. Cassie had insisted I take the front seat, and she climbed in next to Hayes, telling him about how she was going to spend spring break in Aruba, showing him beach photos of her last trip on her iPhone, blah, blah, blah, finding little reasons to squeeze his thigh from time to time, the whole of which I witnessed in the makeup mirror.

"I'd kill to go to Aruba," Fin said. "I have to go to Minnesota with my family. In a car."

Cassie didn't even respond.

I got dropped off at a redbrick house with one sad yellow balloon tied to the doorknob. Joy told me the birthday girl was a six-year-old named Lindsey. Six. That had to be easier than dealing with pretweenies. A frazzled-looking woman answered with a phone in her hand. "Hold on, Kevin!" she yelled into the phone, and then she pulled me into the house. "Thank goodness!" She led me through the living room and showed me a door to the basement. "Go on down. I'll be down in a second." She disappeared into a bathroom.

I stood for a moment, adjusting my cups and fins,

intending to give myself a pep talk, when from behind the closed bathroom door, the woman let loose with a string of swear words that would make a pirate blush. "No, it's not all right, Kevin. I'm sick of your excuses." She said his name as if she were spitting it out. "You're never here, Kevin. It's your daughter's birthday. I know you can't do it for me, but you could do it for her." The smell of cigarette smoke started seeping through the crack below the bottom of the door. I heard crying. "Don't bother coming home, Kevin. I've had it."

I figured the best thing I could do was to keep the kids entertained. The stairs led down to a depressing, low-ceilinged room with a TV, a rug that smelled like cat pee, and some beanbag chairs. *The Little Mermaid* DVD was on, running the scene in which Ariel's father trades his life to set her free of the curse.

The girls weren't watching, though. One girl, the tallest and most conventionally pretty in the room, was holding court. "We can't all be mermaids," she said. "I think Lindsey should be Flounder, and Ruthie and Katie should be Flotsam and Jetsam and — "

The girls caught sight of me at that point and started squealing.

Amazing things, lungs. Tiny ones can produce enough air for really loud noises. The squealing grew even louder, and the girls began to crowd around me.

I began the script. "I've been swimming around all day searching for a special birthday girl to see —"

"Me! I'm Lindsey!" A short girl lunged forward and hugged me. She was adorable — pudgy with a front tooth missing.

"It's Lindsey's birthday," the tall girl said. "It's my birthday in two weeks. And I'm having an even bigger party. I'm getting the princess."

I smiled and made my way over to the middle of the room, the girls still trying to hold on. "Wow. You guys are like barnacles."

Behind me, the tall girl crouched down and peeked under my costume. "She has feet!" More squealing as the tall girl, named Cory, tried to lift up the flounces that served as the fins of my tail.

"Stop that," I said. "Yes, I have feet."

"You don't look like Ariel at all," Cory said, and turned to Lindsey. "This isn't a good one."

Lindsey looked like she was going to cry. If there had been a utility closet nearby, I would have told the mean Cory that it was Ursula's lair and locked her up in it. "I'm not Ariel," I said. "I'm a different mermaid."

"Is that your real hair?" Cory asked. "Because it doesn't look very nice."

I squelched a burning desire to kneel down, look her straight in the eyes, and say: *Is that your real personality? Because it's about as appealing as a sea slug.*

"We're supposed to play a game and get a prize," Cory said. "The Ariel at my cousin's party did that. You've got the stuff in there." She tugged at my bag.

"You are not allowed to touch a mermaid's purse," I said. "That's actually rude."

The girl's face darkened. She turned to Lindsey and said, "Let's have the cake now. This is boring."

Lindsey looked as if she were dying, as if any moment, angels would descend, weeping, to carry her limp soul to heaven. "Okay," she said, and started following Cory up the stairs.

"Everybody, freeze!"

Miraculously, the girls froze. Lindsey looked at me, eyes big and trusting. Something about the way she believed in me, even though I was obviously a fake, gave my fragile ego a boost of vigor and vim. I stood up, adjusted my wig, and grabbed my trident. "I have a proclamation. We're going to play a fun game, and since it's Lindsey's birthday, she gets to go first."

"When it's my birthday, I'm going first," the tall girl said.

"Yeah? Well, that's not today, is it?" I gave her a wicked smile. "After Lindsey, we'll go in order of size. Shortest first and tallest last."

Okay, that was mean, but it was immensely gratifying to see that brat's face when she looked around the room, realizing that she was going to be last.

I turned my attention to Lindsey and let her set out the props for the game and made sure to move the basket close enough that she got it on the first try. I made up a silly song about how wonderful she was and put a string of fake gold pearls around her neck.

Her smile was beautiful.

After the party, I sailed out the door, powerful in a goodness-and-light kind of way, like a mermaid superhero, like maybe I could save the Lindseys of the world from depression, one birthday party at a time.

15

UKE LOVE

Joy handed out our paychecks, and Fin and I squealed like piggies. We had a plan to head straight for the ATM and then the music store. Hayes asked if he could join us, and I was happy to notice that Cassie overheard. Oh, and I made sure to let her know that a wonderful girl named Cory had booked her for a princess party in two weeks. "You'll just love her," I said.

The day was sunny and unnaturally warm for February, a day to make your own dream come true.

The guy at Tenley's rolled his eyes when I walked in the door.

"She has the money!" Fin said.

With a dramatic flourish, I pulled the cash out of my purse — crisp twenties.

He stepped from behind the counter without saying a word and walked over to where the ukes were hanging. No reaction. No congratulations. No whoop or holler. No jig dancing. I guess some people live their lives minimalistically.

He took the one I wanted off the wall and handed it to me.

"Don't you want to play them all?" Hayes asked. "To make sure you get the right one?"

One quick snort came out of Grumpy Gus.

I plucked each string: Mine, mine, mine, mine.

I'd say the sound was like music to my ears, but that wouldn't do it justice.

After I paid, the guy handed me the receipt and my change. The whole thing took less than two minutes.

"That's it?" I was incredulous.

"What did you expect?" the guy asked.

"I don't know . . . to fill out a form . . . or take an oath or a test," I said, "or go through some training process, like you do when you get a driver's license or adopt a baby."

"At the very least, a parade," Hayes added.

"Congratulations," the guy said, and sat on his stool and began leafing through a magazine.

"Thank you for shopping at Tenley's Music Store," Fin said with a slightly wicked smile. "We know you could have purchased this online and appreciate your business."

The guy looked up at Fin with a cold stare, and we left.

"Have a wonderful day," Hayes called back.

I didn't care. I took off the tag that was tied to a tuning peg and started dancing with the uke cradled in my arms.

The guys laughed. "Minerva just got a puppy," Fin said.

Downtown Evanston was hopping. People were out shopping, doing errands. As we walked down Dempster, I strummed a few chords, and the sound of those four strings ringing out in the middle of all that ordinary pedestrian traffic was magical. I could see myself reflected in the store windows: a girl with a uke sticking out of her backpack, walking down the street with her friends. An object can't miraculously make your life perfect, but every time I saw my reflection, I had to smile.

"Stop," Fin said. "Let's busk."

"What's that?" Hayes asked.

"To sing on the street, play for money."

Hayes smiled. "I had no idea there was a word for that."

"*My Fair Lady*," Fin said. "My first musical. I wanted the part of Freddy or Henry Higgins, but I got busker."

I had memorized three songs from the uke songbook that Fin had given me for my birthday. I started to play "Somewhere over the Rainbow." Fin took off the hat he was wearing, set it on the ground in front of us, and started singing harmony with me. Hayes played the part of the appreciative audience by putting a dollar in the hat.

People started smiling at us. A woman stopped and dropped her change into the hat. An old guy gave us the thumbs-up. Hayes joined in singing, and then who should come along? Fin's parents and his two little brothers on their way to get soccer cleats. I am happy to report that they whooped and hollered when they saw us and went crazy over my new baby. Inspired,

I started wailing on the uke, playing this hoedown, old-timey song that I was making up on the fly — spin your partner round and round — and everybody started square dancing.

Sometimes, you have these perfect moments, these moments that are stuffed with a thousand times more life than they can seem to hold; and you want to laugh and cry at the same time because you are so happy, and yet you know the moment is going to end and eventually your soul is going to settle back down.

There was something about singing out there on the street with Fin and Hayes, something about the blue of the sky, something about Fin's parents and brothers dancing, their faces, the way they were just letting it loose, something about having that uke in my arms, the simplicity of the strumming, the fact that all this joy was coming out of four little strings that belonged to me. It got me right in the heart.

Saving my wishes,
Holding my breath,
Outside that window,
Too broke to take that step.

But now I promise
To nail the test,
Take the oath to pursue
My happiness. Oooh.

Finally, I'm right where I want to be.
I'm right where, I'm right where I want
    to be.
Finally, I'm right where I want to be.
Right where I want to be.

Are you that person?
You know the one
Longing to say out loud
What you really want.
You draw a picture,
Show what you need,
Tape it up on the wall
So everybody sees. Oooh.

Finally, you're right where you want
    to be.
You're right where, you're right where
    you want to be.

Finally, you're right where you want
   to be.
Right where you want to be.

Sing the day, sing the sky,
Sing the paycheck, sing the hi.
Drop a dollar in my hat.
Nothing better than that.

Oh! Hey, people
Passing on by,
Consider what you miss
If you keep it quiet.
(Don't keep it quiet, don't keep it quiet.)

Finally, we're right where we want to be.
We're right where, we're right where we
   want to be.
Finally, we're right where we want to be.
Right where we want to be.

16

SCHADENFREUDE

IN THE NEXT DAYS, I could have concentrated on my uke and how fun it was that Fin and I were spending time with a new friend, but that would have been way too healthy.

Minerva, thy name is weakness. I had to go on to Cassie's blog again.

A fresh entry. No comment from Keanu Choy yet.

I'm so excited! The Shedd Aquarium is going to publish one of my photos in their new magazine, so I will officially be a published photographer! The topic of the issue is

seahorse camouflage. Did you know that
seahorses can change their colors and
the patterns of color on their bodies to
match sand or algae or other surroundings?
Camouflage enables them to hide from
predators, but it also makes it easier for them
to ambush their prey! What do they eat?
Teensy tiny shrimp, fish, and plankton.

Much to my dismay, landlover@yahoo.com was
blocked from making any further comments. Rattlefinks
and fudderudder! What's a girl to do? Create a new
account.

deepsee@yahoo.com says:
Congratulations! Did you know that arrogance
can never be camouflaged? It's easy to spot
when you know what to look for!

There is a vocabulary word to describe the twisted
pleasure I got from dropping little bombs on Cassie's
blog: *schadenfreude*. It means feeling joy at someone
else's misfortune. Fin taught it to me. It's German or

Dutch or something. *Schaden* means "shadow" and *Freude* means "joy." Shadowjoy.

It's a terrible thing.

～

Look in all the windows
Of the houses on the street.
Pretty people with pretty secrets
Underneath their feet.
Cigarettes in the bathroom,
Smoke trails out like steam.
Close the door so no one
Hears you scream, hears you scream.

I got a secret.
I got a weakness.
Don't want to feel it.
Keep it, keep it, keep it secret.

My father tiptoed out the door
To never-never land.
My mother gives me gifts that prove
She doesn't understand.

I drop words like bombs online—
That's my evil plan.
No one has to know
Who I am, who I am.

I got a secret.
I got a weakness.
Don't want to feel it.
Keep it, keep it, keep it secret.

Behind the friendly eyes,
Behind the smile,
A shadow hides.
I wonder why there's got to be a dark side.

I got a secret.
I got a weakness.
Don't want to feel it.
Keep it, keep it, keep it secret.

NICE DADS
& EMOTIONAL
DISASTERS

PERHAPS IT WAS the desire to counteract all that negative energy with something positive that drove me to say yes to Fin when he suggested we pool the remainder of our paychecks to buy the FabAb Immediate Results Workout Program and to do the workout the night before our next gig.

The immediate result: abs of ouch and buns of oy.

Once again, you could find us hobbling toward the Get Happy office.

Joy saw us and said, "What now?" Then she noticed

the uke sticking out of my backpack and said, "No way, Minerva. It isn't in the script."

Fin tried to lobby for me, but it was to no avail. Some people simply have no vision. Maybe if I had been able to bring the uke along, things would have gone better, but as Aunt Joan always says: If wishes were horses, we'd all have saddle sores.

Hayes and I were dropped off at a condo complex, one building apart. Joy told us to meet in the middle for the pickup when we were done and gave us extra brochures to hand out, just in case. Luckily the weather was warm, so we didn't need our coats. "Stay in character," she said.

The dad answered. Asian. Smudge of white frosting on his nose. Warm smile. "Let me guess. You're the mermaid?"

"Fins, scales, and all," I said.

"Come in." He led me through a quiet house.

You can walk into some homes and get an immediate bad feeling, and you can walk into others and get this sense of calm. I could tell this was the house of a really nice family just by walking through it. I couldn't put my finger on why. I mean, it wasn't like, ah, the reason is because the sofa is facing southeast, which is the direction of peace.

"My daughter likes three things: soccer, strawberries, and *The Little Mermaid*." He laughed. "If she could play soccer underwater while eating strawberries, she'd be in heaven."

"Soccer is great," I said. "I always wanted to play on a team. But my mom thought participation in any sport would automatically lead to injury, disfigurement, or death."

He laughed. "My wife is the coach!"

A sliding glass door led to the small fenced backyard where a half dozen little girls, all wearing huge soccer jerseys, were chasing after a ball. I guessed the Asian-looking kid with the long black ponytail was his. The blond mom was playing goalie. Luckily mermaids can't play soccer; my gluts and quads would've screamed.

"Game just started. Kids against mom. I'm almost finished. Have a seat." He handed me a strawberry to eat.

The kitchen smelled amazing. On the table was a large, white frosted cake. On it, the outline of a mermaid had been expertly drawn with chocolate icing, the long ponytail filled in. Two sliced strawberries formed the mermaid's bikini top. The dad was now laying more sliced strawberries in a fish-scale pattern to fill in her tail. With extra batter, he had made cupcakes and had drawn seashells and starfish on them with caramel-colored icing.

"That's amazing," I said. "Are you a professional cake baker?"

"No. A graphic designer, but I'll take that as a compliment. I do most of the cooking around here. I love my wife, but she's a bad cook." He made a funny face.

A chorus of cheers and high-pitched laughter came from the girls in the backyard. The mom was on her knees laughing, the girls jumping and high-fiving.

"First goal. Hold on." The dad stood up. "Stay inside so they don't see you yet." He slid open the door, ran out, and cheered. His daughter jumped on him and he spun her around.

"Hey, whose side are you on?" The mom laughed and threw the ball at him.

The dad chased after the ball and kicked it to his daughter. His daughter passed it back to him. He turned sharply and kicked it right past the mom's head into the goal.

The girls went wild. The mom ran out, laughing, and tackled him to the ground. All the girls piled on top.

I looked down at my green-sequined, slippered feet.

Cheers outside. Another goal.

Somewhere, a clock was ticking. A homemade happy-birthday banner was strung on the wall above a trio of framed photographs. The center photo, a serious portrait of the little girl and her parents in front of the lake at sunset, had been altered for the occasion: Someone — the dad? — had taped funny black paper mustaches under their noses and added comic captions. It was silly and cute, and I started to laugh and then some tiny dam inside me broke, and a sudden wave of tears threatened to engulf me. Horrified, I stared at the cupcakes and the cake and tried to push my emotions down.

The mermaid's face looked serene. The lines of chocolate had been applied with a zenlike calm. The strawberries making up her outfit, neatly arranged on that pure white icing, were impossibly red and beautiful and silent.

The dad walked in and must have seen the panic

in my face, because he poured me a glass of water and handed it to me. "Are you . . . okay?"

I stood up, pain from last night's workout shooting through my thighs and abs, and wiped my eyes with the back of my hand. "I should really get this party started — "

"Is there something wrong?"

Outside, the girls were shaking their booties in the cutest victory dance of all time. I wanted to run the other way, but I yanked the sliding door open and started marching out as fast as my fins would allow.

"We thought we'd do this part inside — " he called.

"It's fine," I said, and the girls saw me. As I went through the motions right there on the grass, with my aching muscles and my ill-fitting mermaid suit, the mom and dad kept exchanging *What's going on?* glances. Genuinely nice, the girls played the game even though they could tell I wasn't into it, and I handed out the necklaces and said happy birthday and good-bye, the worst entertainer in the history of Get Happy, Incorporated. Their condo was the last unit in the building, and hoping to make my exit, I walked to the gate on the side of the house.

The dad followed me. "You sure you're all right?"

"Fine. I'm supposed to wait out front until the van comes." I struggled with the latch.

"That doesn't open," he said. "You have to come through the house."

"Well, that's ridiculous," I snapped. "Who would have a gate that doesn't work?"

Awkwardly, with all the girls watching, I followed him in, and he insisted on handing me a seashell cupcake to go, still trying to be courteous in the face of every rude thing I was throwing his way. Embarrassed, I found myself trying to think of one positive thing to say on my way out, and all I could think of was "You have nice window treatments."

He must have thought I was insane.

Outside, I pulled off the stupid red wig and sat — with considerable difficulty — on the curb in front of their condo, hiking my mermaid skirt up and tucking the chiffon flounces of my tail between my legs to hide my crotch. I guess real mermaids don't have to worry about hiding crotches. On top of the muscle ache, my feet were also killing me: The elastic straps of the green sequined ballet slippers were digging into my skin.

To keep from crying, I started digging into the cupcake. A tiny battalion of ants helped distract me by marching in and out of a hill of dirt assembled over a crack in the cement to the right of my feet. The girls had resumed playing outside in the back, their voices rising and falling, no doubt happy that I had left — the foul mermaid who had threatened to darken the day.

"Hey!"

I looked in the other direction to see Hayes walking toward me, a delicious-looking sub in one hand, his button-up Western shirt too short in the sleeves, his bag stuffed with the parts of his costume that he could actually take off: his vest, his gun belt, his hat.

"Is that a mythological sea creature sitting in front of my own two eyes?" he asked, the cheap cowboy boots scuffing in the street. "I didn't know you could breathe out here," he said. "And . . . son of a biscuit, are those feet? What kind of mermaid are you?"

"A washed-up one," I said. "I'm dying. I can't breathe. You finished already, too?"

He dropped his bag and sat down next to me. "The birthday boy hurled chunks."

"You're kidding?"

"Dead serious. They cut the whole party short and gave me a sub. Want a bite? It's germ free. They were individually wrapped."

I showed him my cupcake.

"Seriously, you don't look so good," he said. "Are you okay?"

Everybody was worried about Minerva Watson. I smiled, trying to tell my face not to betray me. His presence was so pure I had to bite my lip to keep from warning him to run as far from me as he could. "I'm peachy."

"Bratty kid?"

I smiled and shrugged. "I'm just a birthday Grinch. I hate birthdays. I always have. My mom always wanted my birthday parties to go a certain way, and they never turned out right."

He stretched out his legs into the street, the toes of his cowboy boots pointing up. "I had great parties."

"Not me. I remember being really little and there was a pile of presents in front of me and every time I opened one, I got a little disappointed because it wasn't what I wanted or it was cheap instead of cool like the ads promised, or something."

He laughed.

I winced. "What I just said sounds really sick, like I'm some kind of selfish person."

"No. You just saw the truth. You were a little truth detector."

It was such a nice thing for him to say.

I pointed down at my friends. "I'm observing a tiny ant city. They are on the move, swarming over this piece of . . . I don't know what it is. . . . Maybe a dead worm? It looks like they're trying to eat it or bring pieces of it back to their lair."

He took a bite of his sandwich and we watched the ants marching. Then he rested a twig near the anthill, and after one ant climbed onto the stick, he moved it over to where the others were swarming. "I'm providing free ant transportation," he said.

"Antportation," I suggested.

He glanced up at me and smiled and then pinched a large crumb from his bread and plopped it near the anthill. Within a few seconds, the ants began to swarm. "That's all it takes for an ant to be happy," he said. "Live it up, little guys."

The scene was kind of disgusting and thrilling

at the same time. The crumb was soon completely covered.

Somebody drove by and slowed down to look at us, and Hayes waved.

"We must look extremely strange," I said. "A cowboy and a mermaid sitting on the side of the road."

"What we do is strange," he said. "But it's kind of fun." He pulled a ten-dollar bill out of his front pocket.

"A tip?"

He grinned. "Cassie was right."

"You flirted?"

"I just complimented the mom on all the party decorations."

I gave the ants a crumb of my cupcake.

Another car drove by and slowed to look.

"It's better than flipping burgers," he said.

"Or Krabby Patties," I said.

He smiled at that, and I couldn't help smiling back. "You almost didn't audition, am I right?" he asked.

"Yeah," I said. "Fin talked me into it."

"He's enthusiastic."

I laughed. "If I recall, you missed some appointment to audition. Dimple doctor?"

He smiled, and his dimples did their cute little thing. "Good memory," he said.

"I was surprised you said yes."

"I wanted a job, but I had no idea I was going to get one that day," he said.

"Yeah, I remember you said getting a job was on your list of things to do."

He handed his sandwich to me and pulled an index card out of his wallet. It was worn, as if he had folded and unfolded it five hundred times. "My list," he said.

"A real list? I thought it was a metaphorical one." I laughed.

He looked a little embarrassed and put it back in his wallet. I felt terrible, because I wasn't laughing at him at all. "I love that idea," I said quickly. "What's on it?"

He just smiled, put his wallet away, and took back his sandwich.

"I will give you the last bite of my cupcake if you tell me the first thing on it," I begged.

His eyes widened and he shook his head. Mouth half full, he managed to say, "Way too embarrassing."

"Okay. Then tell me number two."

He looked up at the sky, considering. His hair, which was slightly curly, had a dent in it from wearing the cowboy hat. He swallowed and wiped his mouth and said: "Number three: Get a job."

"And you got one!"

"Yep."

"What was number two?"

He shook his head, not telling.

I stole what was left of his sandwich and said he had to tell me at least one more thing.

"You're holding my sub hostage?" he asked.

I took a bite out of it.

He laughed. "They'll sound stupid if I say them out loud."

"No, they won't." I took another bite.

"Okay. One more thing and that's it."

I tried to do a drumroll with my feet, but it hurt too much.

He laughed. "Number two: Record some songs."

"That's not stupid. That's cool." I gave him back his sandwich. "So it's a to-do list of positive things, like resolutions?"

He nodded, finishing his sandwich. "I made it on New Year's Eve and gave myself a deadline. I have to do everything on the list before my birthday."

"Which is on . . . ?"

He stretched out his legs and brushed off the crumbs. "May twelfth."

"How many things are on your list?"

"Ten."

"How many things have you done?"

"Three." He laughed.

"Are they all things you can do or are they things like climb Mount Everest or swim across the ocean or star in a major motion picture?"

"They're all things I can do. I just have to get up the nerve."

The van pulled up with Cassie in the front seat. Joy unrolled the window, a foul look on her face. "Minerva, get up off that curb. Why the halo are you sitting in the dirt? And, Hayes, you should be wearing the rest of your costume. You should be in character!"

Why the halo. Almost as good as *son of a biscuit*. Fin was going to love it.

Hayes pulled me to my feet, and we got in the van. Joy huffed and drove to the next house in silence.

Fin was waiting outside, standing on the curb in full pirate regalia with ketchup all over his frilly shirt.

"Well, I think we've all arrived at a very special

place," he said with his Jack Sparrow voice, tumbling into the van. "Spiritually, musically, and — "

"What happened?" Joy's voice snapped.

"Just a wee food fight."

Joy slammed her hands against the steering wheel. "I do not want to hear that! Why the halo can't — "

"We all be like Cassie?" I blurted out.

"Yes!" Joy said, obviously lacking the sarcasm gene. "She follows the script and she keeps her costume clean and gets consistent referrals from her parents."

Cassie didn't say a word, and Fin, Hayes, and I traded guilty smiles.

Joy held up a business card. "Another mom was at Cassie's party and she wants to book her for next month. That's what I need. Thank the Lord!" She turned to us and gave us a triumphant *harrumph*.

18

SOMETHING
GOOD

FIN, HAYES, AND I started hanging out together. Hayes even helped with the script writing and filming of our annual Fin and Min Show, something we'd been doing since we were seven. In honor of our employment at Get Happy, we decided this year's show would be an original stop-action musical. It is called *Get Unhappy: Billy's Birthday Party Goes Bad*, starring a hapless marshmallow bunny and his marsh mallow-chick friends, which quickly turns violent when the Get Happy entertainer — an evil-looking ceramic rabbit wearing a paper pirate hat — goes off script. Peeps without heads, peeps cut in half, peeps hanging by their necks. We had no problem finding lots of pastel props and scenery because my mother had decorated every inch of our house for Easter, and I "borrowed" a number of choice items while she was at work. The filming took two weeks, because we got ridiculously elaborate, and Hayes added a score and all these cool sound effects. The screening party was awesome — at Fin's house, of course, since we do everything at Fin's house because my mom wouldn't be able to tolerate the mess — and Fin served vim and vigor juice.

Eventually, spring break rolled around. My vacation began with a text from Fin on my phone when I woke up. He had sent it at something like 6 A.M.

Have been on the road an hour already.
I will never make my children get up this early.

He was driving to Minnesota to visit his grand-parents. Cassie was in Aruba. Hayes and I were both spending the break at home. Hayes had a brother in college who was coming home for the week, and it sounded like he was looking forward to seeing him.

My mom wasn't taking time off work, so I was giddy at the thought of having a week to sit around in my jammies, playing my uke and drawing little diagrams of the chords I made up so that I could remember what I liked.

Maybe some people need to go to Aruba, I thought, *but this is enough for me.*

Business was slow at Get Happy, but Hayes and I did have gigs that first Sunday of the break. It was odd being the only ones in the dressing rooms and in the van.

"So what are you two doing with your days off?" Joy asked as we drove to the first gig. I was sitting in the front with her, and Hayes was in the back.

"Minerva's coming over tomorrow," Hayes said. "I'm going to help her record one of her songs." I turned around and looked at him, and he smiled and tipped his hat.

"On that little mandolin you play?" Joy asked me.

Hayes leaned forward. "It's a ukulele. She writes her own songs. I'm going to record her doing uke and vocals, and I'll add bass and maybe some percussion — "

"That sounds productive," Joy said.

"Yep," he said. "She's coming over at noon and bringing her uke."

I flipped down the visor and looked at Hayes in the mirror.

"And Hayes is cooking lunch," I said. "A special gourmet lunch. With a really delicious chocolate dessert."

"He is?" Joy exclaimed. "That is wonderful. Most boys don't even know how to boil water."

"Belgian chocolate fondue, I believe is what he said was for dessert, right, Hayes?" I turned around.

Hayes laughed. "Yep."

I hardly remember anything about those gigs. I kept wondering if he was serious about me coming on Monday, and I wasn't sure if I wanted him to be or not because it sounded fun and also scary. When the day was over and we were driving back to headquarters, I was too chicken to say anything about it, and he didn't say a word. After we had changed out of our costumes and were walking to the elevator, he told me about something that had happened at his last party, none of which I heard because I was trying to work up the courage to just ask him.

The elevator doors opened and he pulled out his cell phone. He started texting someone, which I thought was kind of rude, and I pushed the button for the lobby.

A moment later, he put his phone away, and my phone buzzed.

A text from Hayes.

"I thought you might need my address," he said.

The doors opened.

"See you at noon," he said, and held the building door for me. "Don't forget your uke."

"Okay," I heard myself say. I must have walked out because I did arrive home that day.

~

WHEN I AM A parent, no matter how freaked out I am about stuff, I am never going to show it so my kid won't know that I'm worried and won't hide everything from me. My mom would have freaked out if I had told her I was going over to a boy's basement during spring break to play music while she was at work; she would have wanted a background check on Hayes and would have wanted to install surveillance cameras. So I didn't tell her.

The next day, I woke up early and made cupcakes

because I was anxious and needed something to do. Then I ceremoniously ripped the ruler off the cookie tin of my fake uke — you served me well, O Makeshift Plaything — and put a dozen cupcakes in the tin. I tried on six outfits, finally decided on one, and rode over to Hayes's house on my bike, the cupcakes and uke in my backpack.

Knock. Knock.

He smiled.

I was nervous, so I pretended to trip on my way in, and he laughed.

"Cupcakes," I said.

"Thank you," he said, taking the tin. "But I'm crushed. You didn't trust me to provide a special gourmet lunch?"

He brought me into the kitchen. On the table were — this was adorable — peanut butter and jelly sandwiches on white bread, cut in triangles, and those little chocolate Easter eggs wrapped in foil.

He put some chocolate eggs in my hand. "If we hold them long enough, they'll melt and then we'll have . . ."

"Fondue?"

He smiled.

We sat and ate and talked. He told me that his dad was a librarian, brainy and hilarious, and that his brother was home from college, but hanging out with his old high school friends. No mention of where his mother was, and I didn't ask.

Every house has a different vibe. The only word I can think of to describe the Martinelli house: *male*. Very brown and plain and comfortable. No knick-knacks, but piles of books everywhere. No tablecloths. No scented candles. There were cartoons taped to the bathroom mirror, and funny photos of him and his brother on the fridge. After lunch, he led me through the living room and down the stairs into the basement, where there was a pool table and a desk with a bunch of recording equipment.

I'm sure I said something brilliant, like "Cool."

"This is basically where I live," he said, and showed me his various basses and recording equipment.

I pulled out my uke and my songwriting journal.

Hayes set up a microphone and we started recording.

Let me tell you, recording is hard. As soon as you hit that red RECORD button, you automatically tense up.

Whenever Hayes would signal me to start, I'd make a mistake. I was getting embarrassed and frustrated and sure that Hayes was regretting his offer. Finally, he leaned back and said, "Just sing it once all the way through to remind yourself how it goes. I won't record."

I closed my eyes and sang and played without making any noticeable mistakes, and as soon as I got to the end, I stood up and screamed: "Son of a biscuit! Why couldn't I do that when we were recording?"

Hayes grinned. "I *was* recording!"

Genius.

Right after that, our phones both signaled an incoming text at the same time.

Fin.

Parents too cheap to stop for lunch. Inhaling
pizza-flavored goldfish to stay alive. Arrrgh.

Attached was a picture of him and his youngest brother, Sammy, taken with a fish-eye app. Their noses were gigantic, and goldfish crackers were sticking out of their nostrils.

We laughed so hard we cried.

HAYES CALLED ME the next day.

"Just say yes or no," he said.

"Yes," I said. "What did I say yes to?"

"To coming with me to do something on my list."

"Oooh! Where to?"

We met at the Davis El station. My mom hated the El, said it was unsafe. The only other times I had been on it was with Fin and his dad. Two years in a row, his dad took us to see a musical downtown for Fin's birthday.

If you've never taken a train anywhere, subway or regular, put it on your list. You stand on the platform, waiting, and then you see it approaching from the distance. When the train arrives and you climb into it, you can't help feeling like you're going somewhere, not to a destination but to a destiny.

Hayes gave me the window seat. I liked looking out at everything passing by. In some places, the train went close to an apartment building or a house, and you could see inside people's windows. In other places, it was running alongside the rooftops, and you could see exhaust fans and graffiti tags and fire escape ladders. The train stopped lots of times, and each time, I looked at Hayes to see if we were getting off. Finally, I settled back to enjoy the scenery, except, at that point in our ride, the neighborhood was sad: boarded-up buildings, trash all over the platforms, and a guy passed out next to a doorway, with a newspaper covering his face.

As people got on and off, Hayes kept checking them out. "We just need to find the right — "

"Drug dealer to buy from?" I whispered.

He laughed.

"The right liquor store to rob?" I asked.

He shook his head.

"The right prostitute — " I stopped and punched him lightly. "Tell me that is not on your list."

He laughed.

At the next stop, a little kid got on, sat by himself in one of the yellow plastic seats, opened up a book, and started reading. About eight years old riding the El alone in this neighborhood.

Hayes smiled. "I found my first man," he whispered. "We're getting off at the next stop. Be ready."

When I tried to get him to explain what he was

going to do, he kept shushing me; his legs were jiggling and he was cracking his knuckles as if his adrenaline was pumping.

As the train pulled up to the next station, Hayes stood up and, without hesitating, stuck a crisp ten-dollar bill between the pages of the boy's book. The kid looked up, shocked, but Hayes kept walking out the door. I followed and turned back to see the kid's face as the train pulled away. Wild joy. Hayes had the same expression.

"You just gave a kid ten bucks? That was on your list? A random act of kindness?"

He laughed. "It's trite, isn't it? But it felt really good." He started jumping around on the platform like a boxer loosening himself up. "Really good."

"I wish a stranger would've handed me ten bucks when I was a kid."

"*That* is my point," he said. "That kid will grow up with a good attitude, thinking something good could happen any day."

I punched him again.

"What's that for?" he asked.

"For going all Mother Teresa on me."

He laughed, pulled out his wallet, and showed me two more crisp tens. "You get to pick the next one."

"Really?"

I took the ten, excited. A new train rumbled in and opened its doors for us.

~

THE LAST DAY of the break, Friday, we did another thing from Hayes's list. It was after we had spent a few days recording. I called my mom and made up a story about how Joy had messed up the schedule and I was on for two gigs: one at five and one at seven. Hayes had all the supplies ready, and as we walked to the corner of Davis and Sherman, he described this article he'd read about a guy who went on a sort of happy campaign in Washington, DC. "He and his friends stood on a busy street corner at rush hour and held up signs to make passing motorists smile," he said.

"Just the phrase *passing motorist* makes me smile," I said. "Did it work?"

Hayes stopped in front of a burger joint. "We'll find out." He tore open a package of poster board and took out two markers.

"So . . . ," I said. "What do we put on the signs?"

"Anything that'll make somebody honk or smile or laugh or wave. We want to try to get as many people as we can to respond in the next hour." He balanced the stack of poster boards on a fire hydrant. A steady stream of cars rushed by. "What would make somebody happy just reading it?"

My mind went blank.

"A phrase," he said. "Like *Cheer up*, only more original."

"How about *Try robust enthusiasm*?"

He laughed and wrote in large letters:

> *Try robust enthusiasm today!*

We took turns writing down our ideas.

> *Honk if you love chocolate.*
> *Hey, beautiful . . . yeah, you!*
> *Grab life by the ears.*
> *Honk if you love someone.*
> *Passing motorists rock!*
> *Seize the second.*

"Ready?" he asked.

I nodded.

We each took a sign, leaned the rest against the hydrant, stood on the curb, and held up our messages.

A car went by and the driver did a funny double take.

We both laughed. "Well," I said. "It'll work for us if nothing else."

"She smiled!" He pointed and waved at the next car and then the next. "Him, too."

The honks started coming.

A guy in a suit walked by and gave us a huge smile and a thumbs-up.

Hayes looked at me. "It's going to be hard to keep count."

A truck approached. "Trucks count for double," I said, waving my sign and reaching up to pull on my imaginary horn.

The guy honked, and Hayes started jumping and hooting in a hilarious way. Two women walking on the other side of the street stopped to laugh. The whole thing was incredibly cheesy, but you wouldn't believe how fun it was. For the next hour, we made what seemed like all of Evanston happy. Motorists. Cabbies.

Truck drivers. Moms pushing strollers. Joggers. An old guy with a cane. Every honk, smile, or wave was like a shot of positive energy coming back at us.

As we were packing up our signs, the owner of the burger joint actually came out and invited us to come in for free burgers and fries. When we were done, who should walk by but little Lindsey, the adorable six-year-old I rescued from the mean girl in that basement, and her mom. The mom was talking on her cell phone, with little Lindsey walking two steps behind her, wearing leotards and — get this — the fake gold pearls from her party around her neck. Lindsey's eyes lit up when she realized who I was and she pulled on her mom's sweater. "It's her," she whispered.

Her mom gave me one of those distracted nodding smiles.

"Hi, Lindsey," I said. "You look beautiful with your necklace. Are you just coming from a ballet lesson?"

She nodded, wide-eyed and smiling, so thrilled that I remembered her name, and pulled at her mom's shirt again. Her mom recognized me and lowered the phone for a second. "Oh, look who it is! Linz already requested you for next year's birthday party." I could tell she wondered what Hayes and I were doing with those signs, but she went back to her cell conversation, her smile dropping. "You need to pick her up tomorrow at nine, Kevin. That's what we agreed on." She pulled Lindsey along, but Lindsey kept looking back at me, her little legs pudgy and pink, her eyes full of admiration.

"One of your fans?" Hayes asked.

I nodded.

Joy Banks and Cassie Lott could eat that with a side of fries.

We got our food and walked down Church Street toward Northwestern, talking and eating.

The day had been overcast, but now it was clearing and the sun was setting. We crossed Sheridan Road and took a trail through some trees, and the ground became sandy, and suddenly, there it was in all its glory . . . the lake. No matter how often I see it, I am always amazed by how big it is. When I was little, I called it Michigan Ocean. That evening, in the fading light, the water was a beautiful greenish gray, the waves small and gentle, the water folding right at the shore, as though each wave were happy to come home.

We took off our shoes and walked in the cold, damp sand as far as we could one way, talking and stopping to skip rocks, then we turned around and walked back and sat on the sand facing the lake, the only people left on the beach, the sky now dark.

"So do you know Ray's?" he asked.

I shook my head.

"It's over on Prairie Avenue. It's this old house where they have live music. They have open mics one Saturday each month."

"That sounds cool," I said, already getting nervous.

"So . . ." He smiled at me.

"Is this on your list?" I asked.

He nodded. "Say yes. We can do a duet."

"When?"

"Next Saturday, April fifteenth."

The date came with a shadow attached to it, which flickered across my mind. It was the date of Keanu Choy's lecture, but I decided it was a perfect day to play music with Hayes.

"Okay," I said. "I'll do it." He fist-bumped me, and I added, "If you get a reward for doing everything on that list of yours, I want a piece of it."

He laughed.

I looked out at the lake. The half-moon lit a path on the water, leaving the rest black and mysterious.

"What made you start your list in the first place?" I asked.

He shrugged. "I was depressed. My brother left for college, and my parents split up. School was stressful. I hated being there, but I hated coming home because my mom had taken all this stuff with her and it didn't feel like home anymore." He picked up a rock and tossed it.

"Where is she?"

"In Waukegan."

"Did she just leave out of the blue?"

"No. They were fighting. She said they tried." He smiled and shrugged again.

"Did you get a choice about whether to go with her or stay with your dad?"

He nodded. "I didn't want to move. School was bad enough here. It would have been worse to move."

"So at some point, you got the idea to make the list?"

"I got tired of being depressed and — there's that

whole New Year's resolution thing that people do — so I decided to make a list and gave myself a deadline. I figured if I started doing something, I'd feel better."

"It's working, right?"

Hayes smiled. "Yeah."

"I'm glad." I dug my toes into the cold sand. We sat quiet for a few moments, listening to the lapping of the water against the shore. Way out in the distance, a speck of light from a boat danced in the dark, and to the right, Chicago lights glowed. "So what's left on the list?"

He turned and smiled, and even though his features were dark, I felt a rush of heat move from his eyes straight into my own. "I don't know if I'm ready to confess," he said. "After the open mic, I'll only have one thing left to do, but it's kind of scary. . . ."

"Scary? I didn't think you were scared of anything."

"Me? Not scared? You've got to be kidding. I'm scared."

"You are not. You walk up to people and shake their hands, you audition for jobs, you put on cowboy suits and face small children, you sing in the street, you do good deeds. You're the most together person I know."

"I was terrified to shake your hand, terrified at that

audition, terrified when we were all in that van driving to the first party, terrified to sing with you and Fin on the street."

"You were not."

"I was." He looked out at the lake. "You're the one who's not afraid of anything."

I laughed. "Me? I am filled to the brim with fear."

"Minerva Watson? You're kidding? You and Fin do what you want. You're known for that."

"And I am secretly an internal wreck," I said. "If you could see the real me, you'd be horrified."

"Let me see. . . ." He leaned in, with this joking expression, as if he were trying to see the real me in the dark through the portals of my eyes. I made a funny expression and leaned in closer, too, as if I were trying to peer through the darkness to a deeper Hayes. Then his face softened and the moonlight flickered in his eyes. I stopped breathing. My body was sitting on the sand, but my soul or my spirit or whatever you want to call it was traveling through the light of his eyes and really seeing him.

Then I panicked and started doing the Get Happy song and dance. He laughed and let the moment go.

My phone buzzed, and it was my mom, worried because it was getting late. While I was calming her down, Hayes got out his phone and whispered that he was calling his dad to ask him to drive me home.

"I'm getting a ride home, Mom," I said. "I'll see you in, like, half an hour."

Hayes made his call and agreed on a pick-up spot with his dad. We said good-bye to the lake and walked back to Sheridan Road and hung out there, talking and waiting.

Right as the car pulled up, Hayes stopped me, and said, "Wait." And then he made me hold out my hand.

"Your plakette, my lady," he said, and dropped a warm smooth stone into my palm.

He held open the car door for me, and when I got in, his dad turned around and — big smile — shook my hand.

In the car, he gave his dad a hard time about what he was listening to on the radio and they teased each other about it in a cute way. I sat in the back and held myself very still, watching the moon follow us home.

Once, when I was six or seven, we took a trip to my aunt Joan's ranch and — I remember this moment vividly — she brought a candy dish down from a high shelf and held it in front of me and said, "Take as many as you want, Minerva." The dish was full of perfectly smooth round candies in pastel colors, and I scooped up a handful and walked around, holding myself very still so that I wouldn't lose a single one.

~

JUST SAYING

I want to make a list
Of all the things I don't want to miss—
This journey full of sudden turns
    and twists.
You got one of your own.
Your resolutions down in a row.
Come on and show me what you wrote, I
    want to know.

Someday the writing's gonna fade away.
We gotta move before it goes.

Something good, something new,
Something out of the blue,

Something untried and true,
Something big to see you through,
Something long overdue.
It could happen to me and you.

Let's get on the next train,
Ride the busy rhythm on through the day,
Watch for signs and let our own rules
  decide the way.
Fate could take you and me,
Throw us out on some random street.
Strangers we meet could change our
  destiny.

There are cracks in the sidewalk,
I think they're meant to be.

Something good, something new,
Something out of the blue,
Something untried and true,
Something big to see you through,
Something long overdue.
It could happen to me and you.

I'm at the very beginning.
I may be losing or may be winning.
While I'm on the solid ground, my head
 is spinning.
But in a quiet room
I'll find the time to heal the wound,
Grab a line and hold it tight to pull
 me through.
We got to keep this world we're on
From sinking down too soon.

Something good, something new,
Something out of the blue,
Something untried and true,
Something big to see you through,
Something long overdue.
It could happen to me and you.

19

WHAT'S HIDDEN DOESN'T STAY HIDDEN

BACK TO SCHOOL. Fin was a hyper, nervous pogo stick of energy because he was auditioning for the play *Our Town* and he desperately wanted the part of George Gibbs, one of the leads. While he was busy after school, I got together with Hayes to rehearse for the open mic. And here's the thing: I didn't tell Fin about any of it. It's not as if it were a terrible secret, but I knew that a little part of him would feel left out, and I didn't want to throw anything at him — even something as small as me and Hayes singing together — during the whole audition process. He was called back for the second round of auditions on Thursday. On Friday the director asked just four people to come back for an absolute final read-through. Fin's fingernails were bitten to near oblivion.

After school that day when I arrived home, I remember it smelled as if a giant vat of cleanser had permeated the cells of everything in the house. My mom had flipped her schedule, traded with her coworker so she had today off and would be working tomorrow. Cleaning the house was Pat Watson's idea of a day off.

I called out a quick hello — she was rummaging in the utility room — and ran upstairs to think of a way to make things better with Fin. My room was a picture of order. The top of my dresser was clean, every drawer closed, the mess on my desk gone. My bed was made, Aunt Joan's puffy patchwork quilt stored away and replaced with the thinner, store-bought bedspread and matching sheets that I never liked.

At first, I didn't think much of it. My mother had done major cleans in the past. And then I remembered the necklace.

I dove to look under the bed.

Nothing. The rug was a blank landscape. In the closet, all my shoes were neatly stacked on a shoe rack, my favorites next to the ones I never wore, and no sheepherder boots among them.

My mom appeared in the doorway. "Hi, sweetie. How was your —"

I tried to keep the panic out of my voice. "Mom, what did you do?"

"'Thank you' would be a more appropriate response, Minerva. Your room was a disaster zone."

"Did you throw stuff away?" I looked under the bed again, hoping that the boots would miraculously reappear. "Mom? Did you actually throw things away?"

"I have been asking you every day for the past year to clean your room. Look at how cute that dresser looks without a pile of —"

"Where did you put everything?"

"It's trash day. I threw away the trash and put everything else in a bag for Goodwill —"

"Where's the Goodwill bag?"

"In the kitchen."

"Are my boots there, those brown ones you hated that I got last year?"

"They were filthy."

A hot wall of anger was rising up inside me; in my peripheral vision, the room seemed to be turning red. "Did you throw them out?"

"They were absolutely not worth saving."

"Where's the trash?"

"Minerva, those boots — "

"Is it gone? Did they pick up the trash?" I already knew the answer.

"For heaven's sake, Minerva. You're being ridiculous."

I lashed out. "You don't have the right to mess with my things."

She looked as if I had slapped her. "Minerva, I don't like this attitude. That is the last time I clean your room. You can live in a pig sty!" She left in a huff.

I ran downstairs and double-checked the garbage can. I scoured our yard and then our street, just to make sure that the necklace hadn't fallen out. I dumped everything out of the Goodwill bag and went through each item, in case it had gotten tangled up in something else.

After twenty minutes of searching, I had to face the fact that it was gone.

I went back up to my room and stood there,

surrounded by the immaculate order: the smooth bed-spread, the gleaming mirror, the parallel vacuum lines on the rug.

I pictured the seahorse, the curl of the tail around the black silk cord, and I pictured my dad's handwriting in black ink on the cream-colored card.

> *I know that gifts are a far cry from being*
> *there all these years, but I want you to know that*
> *I am always thinking about you. I don't know if*
> *it's your style, but I hope you like it.*

The necklace was mine. I was supposed to decide if I should sell it or throw it away or maybe even someday wear it and feel the weight and elegance of it against my skin. He had finally given me something I could look at and hold in my hand. It had arrived without warning, and now, just as suddenly, it was gone.

The universe giveth and the universe sweepeth away, and your needs, your desires, your feelings are swept away, too.

I looked at myself in the mirror. No black silk cord around my neck. No silver and pearl-studded beauty against my skin. Nothing but a hollow, silent cry inside my throat.

I COULD NOT EVEN look at my mother.

I may not have been learning as much about history or math or biology as I could have, but I was learning the valuable lesson of how to completely ignore the existence of another human being while living in the same town house. My mom and I spent the entire evening in our separate bubbles. She didn't insist that I sit across from her at the dinner table, and I didn't ask if I could eat in front of the television. I loaded up my plate and cushioned myself on the couch.

I texted Fin, asking him to call, and he wasn't calling back. Nothing good was on. I flipped through the channels, knowing it would be better for my soul if I went upstairs and played the uke, but I couldn't move.

I texted again: Where are you? I'm going through something big and I really need to talk.

My phone buzzed. Text from Fin: I didn't get the part. Thanks for asking.

I had completely forgotten about his final audition. I set my phone on the coffee table, got up, and paced. I wanted to throw something.

Sounds were coming from the kitchen, dishes clunking angrily into the dishwasher.

I grabbed my phone and texted back. I'm sorry, Fin. Please call.

No call.

Over the next two hours, I texted five apologies. No reply.

Silence is a terrible thing. Hoping that he had just turned off his phone and that he wasn't that mad, I stormed into my room and dove under the covers.

I woke up in the middle of the night feeling sick to my stomach. Too much was happening at once. I went into the kitchen and stared at the clock. I couldn't think of a way to make things right with Fin, and I couldn't stop thinking about the necklace. My father had reached out to me, and no matter how much I told myself that I was putting him out of my mind, I couldn't. Finally, I sat at the computer. I thought for a long time, and then I called up Google images. I typed in *Keanu and Minerva*.

I deleted it.

I typed it in again.

I walked away.

I came back.

I stared at it.

I hit IMAGE SEARCH.

I held my breath, and a thumbnail picture popped onto the screen. I clicked to enlarge it.

A photograph. There we are. He is standing in front of a large circular blue aquarium tank, holding me. I'm about one. I've got that wispy black baby hair and my eyes are huge and I'm wearing a striped dress and little black shoes that I've seen in other photos. Whoever took this photo must have been kneeling, because the angle shows a beautiful ceiling above our heads, lit with blue lights. We are surrounded by blue, as if we are in the water. No wonder I fantasized that he'd emerge from the lake at the beach when I was little.

I clicked on the link to see where the photo lived, and it took me to an archive of Shedd Aquarium newsletter articles going back twenty years. Caption:

KEANU AND MINERVA ENJOY
THE FACULTY HOLIDAY PARTY.

He is holding me with one arm as if he's having fun showing me off. He is young. We both look happy. My chubby arm is resting on his shoulder so casually. At one point in my life, I was completely comfortable in his arms.

I printed it out.

20

THE SHEDD
AQUARIUM

I WOKE UP light-headed; my movements felt involuntary, as if I had stepped into a strong current and was being carried along.

I put on my green dress and took my uke, the photo, and my backpack downstairs. My mom was already at work, although it was Saturday, because she had not worked the day before. The note on the counter, reminding me about assignments that I hadn't done that week, had a tone of annoyance. I rode my bike to the El station and took a train to Chicago.

When I left the train, it took me a while to figure

out which way to walk, the sun bouncing off everything so brightly it hurt to look ahead. After a long walk, I could see the aquarium, which looked like a Greek temple with the magnificent lake behind it and a cloudless blue sky above it.

Huge and majestic, the building had four pillars and colorful banners between each pillar, announcing special exhibits. The banner on the right read: SEAHORSE SECRETS. At the top of the stairs near the entrance, a glossy cardboard cutout of a seahorse — six feet tall — was on display. Next to it was a large poster explaining my dad's award and his research. The reality of him hit me: My dad, the guy I had tried and failed to avoid thinking about for so many years, was right here, in this building.

The line to get in was out the door. I stood behind the last family waiting and checked my wallet. I hadn't done my research to find out how much it cost to get in. When the line finally reached the doors, the ticket prices were visible. More than I expected. I left to find an ATM, tapped out what was allowed to be withdrawn, and hurried back. By the time I walked in, I was out of breath.

The main room, the grand rotunda, was the same room that was in the photo I had in my backpack. The same beautiful blue ceiling and curved aquarium tank. I had been here fifteen years ago in my dad's arms — we had been at a party together, and he had been showing me off. When he moved here again to work and saw this, it must have brought back memories of us together. I wondered if he wrote the letter to me here, in the beauty and peace of this aquarium.

Inside the first large tank, the scene was mesmerizing, plants and animals moving underwater gracefully and effortlessly: sea turtles, moray eels, and parrot fish. A little girl standing with both hands on the glass was literally yelping with excitement every time a creature swam by.

The mom asked if I would mind taking a picture of the family together.

I held up the camera. Inside the frame, the parents stood, all smiles, with their daughter between them. "Say 'fishies,' Zoe!" the mom said.

I started to get a little panicky and walked around for a while, not looking at the tanks, with an internal debate raging in my head. Should I play it safe and go home right now or should I go into the auditorium and at least stay for the lecture? I didn't have to approach him; I could just sit in the back, a baby step to be in the same room at the same time. If he happened to see me and recognize me after the lecture, I could make it sound as though it wasn't a big deal, tell him that my bio teacher had recommended coming. He'd see the uke in my backpack and ask me about it. I'd have something to say. Yes, I play the uke. I'm doing an open mic later tonight with a friend. I'm doing just fine, thank you, as you can see.

I made my way to the auditorium doors. People were streaming in. A man wearing a blue suit asked for my ticket.

I showed him my receipt.

"That's your admission to the aquarium," he said. "You had to reserve a lecture ticket in advance." He looked past me to take the reservations of a couple waiting behind me.

I just stood there.

"Sorry," he said. "Your ticket does give you admission to the seahorse exhibit as well as our permanent exhibits."

Stunned, I walked away. The corridor was crowded, full of moms and dads and strollers. I walked into a bathroom to escape. There were three women waiting for the stalls, and I squeezed past them and stood at the sink. The soap was pink and foamy. I glanced up at the mirror just as one of the stall doors behind me opened. Cassie Lott walked out.

"Minerva!" she squealed, and stepped up to the sink next to me. "Look at you with your uke! How fun! What are you doing here? Are you going to the lecture?"

Of course she would be here. I don't know why I was surprised. I rinsed the soap off my hands. Words came out: "My bio teacher wanted us to come, but I didn't reserve a space." I heard myself laugh at my own stupidity.

"It's packed!" she said. "If I had known you were coming, I could have saved you a seat up front with us." She leaned over the sink to wash her hands, and a pendant that had been stuck under her shirt came free and swung forward.

I stopped midbreath.

It was a seahorse. It was *my* seahorse on a black silk cord.

My mind tried to make sense of it. Perhaps the

necklace had fallen out of the garbage truck, and, in the strangest of all coincidences, Cassie found it on the street. Or maybe a friend of hers found it, and knowing that she loves seahorses, gave it to her. I asked, full of genuinely innocent wonder, "Where did you get that?"

She lifted the pendant and smiled. "This? My stepdad." She let it go and pulled lip gloss out of her back pocket and leaned even closer to the mirror to put it on. "He's the one giving the lecture." She smiled at herself and smacked her lips. "Didn't you know that? Keanu Choy."

My stomach dropped, and the color must have drained from my face because she asked if I was okay. A stall opened up. Fortunately, the line was gone, so I turned and walked in. As I twisted the lock, I managed to mumble something about how I had eaten something that was making me feel sick.

Through the crack in the door, I saw her finish up in the mirror. "Sorry," she said. "Hey, do you want me to see if I can get you in?"

"No," I said.

"Okay. I have to go. Hope you feel better. See you next Saturday."

She left and more people came in. I stood in the stall, staring at the door, feeling as if the room were tilting back and forth.

Images were flashing through my mind. A young Cassie and her divorced mom living in California. Cassie and her mom hanging out at the beach. Cassie and her mom meeting Keanu Choy, hitting it off, having so much in common. Vacations together. A marriage. Trips to Hawaii, Fiji, Bermuda. The job offer in Chicago. The decision to move. Enrolling Cassie in Parker, nothing but the best.

Through the crack, I saw a mom and her kids lining up at the sinks, two girls and a little boy. "What did you like best, guys?" the mom asked.

"The seahorses," one daughter said.

"The rays," the second one said.

"The hot dogs," the boy said, and the mom laughed.

Someone from the line knocked on my door.

"I'll be out in a minute," I said.

A little kid in the stall next to me was talking to her mom nonstop.

I walked out of the stall, avoiding eye contact, washed my hands, and left. The doors to the auditorium were closed and a sign read: LECTURE IN PROGRESS. A red velvet rope blocked the entrance.

I turned to leave and thought I was headed to the aquarium exit, but I was funneled into an S-shaped room lined with small tanks, photos, and facts on every wall. The Save Our Seahorse special exhibit. The last place I wanted to be.

Moms and dads and kids and single people were all shuffling along, waiting their turns to get closer to the tanks, or stopping to read the stuff on the walls, or listening to the recorded tour on their smartphones.

A different species of seahorse was in each tank. The creatures looked powerless and sad, with their tails curled around strands of seaweed or floating through the water, their faces expressionless, their bodies rigid, even when moving, their bony plates like primeval armor: tiny, armless, aimless toy soldiers.

Hot, unable to breathe, I pushed against the flow, trying to get out in the direction that people were coming in. As I was entering the last curve of the room, the only opening in the flow of people was closest to the wall. On it was a display explaining the SOS Project, with photos from my dad's research and dives. The time line was in reverse for me, so as I moved forward, my dad was getting younger in the pictures. There was a photo of a whole group wearing SOS polo shirts on a large sailboat with Keanu in the center, and a younger Cassie was in the shot with what looked like her mom standing next to her.

I kept moving forward, not wanting to look at the photos but unable to look away. The last photo stopped me. It was the same picture I had printed out and brought with me, the picture of my young dad and me surrounded by the blue of the grand rotunda, except they had cropped me out. The picture was just a head shot of my dad, and the caption said, SOS FOUNDER KEANU CHOY AT SHEDD DURING HIS INTERNSHIP.

If you looked very closely, you could see that my chubby little arm on his shoulder had been erased.

Something inside me, some inner rope that had been holding me, snapped. I took the printed photo out of my backpack and threw it away. Then I walked from the exhibit to the lecture hall. The museum guard who had been standing in front of the auditorium doors was gone. I unhooked the velvet rope and simply walked in.

The stage was lit up with a projected image of seahorses, and there he was, talking. Keanu Choy.

I stepped to the side and stood against the back wall.

He was handsome and confident, wearing black jeans, a crisp white shirt, and a headset microphone, walking around the stage and using his arms to punctuate his remarks with robust enthusiasm, sleek, graceful, the kind of man who never trips over a word or a crack in the sidewalk.

"Thanks to the efforts of marine conservationists, more seahorse habitats are being protected, but we still have a long way to go, my friends. For those of you who are divers, please help us by contributing to our seahorse survey project. If you see a seahorse in the wild, be a marine detective. Try to notice everything you can — weather conditions, habitat, size of the seahorse, distinguishing marks, spots, speckles, stripes . . . behavior — Is it clinging to a holdfast? Is it holding an umbrella?"

Everybody laughed.

"Send us your description and a photo or video." He smiled. "Make sure you use an underwater camera, though!"

More laughter.

"Seriously, though, if you do photograph seahorses, please, please refrain from excessive flash, and if they move away, let them go. Like many of us, they don't want their faces to be plastered all over YouTube." More laughter. "Protecting and preserving these creatures is always our main goal. Questions?"

A woman in a navy blue aquarium blazer stepped forward and invited anyone with a question to stand at either of two microphones that were set up toward the back of each aisle. Several people lined up.

"Dr. Choy, I loved your talk and found it so interesting that the male delivers the babies, so to speak," a woman gushed. "You said that the father carries the fertilized eggs in his pouch. Do they have many partners or do they mate for life?"

"Seahorses often mate for life." He smiled. "They don't swim in schools, the way other fish do. They are generally loners, but they have this beautiful little ritual. Every morning, the female visits her male mate. They just hang out together. It's like mom and dad eating breakfast and reading the paper."

More laughter.

He held up his hand. "And here's the sweetest part.

They often change to a brighter color when they are together. Beautiful, right?"

The audience loved it.

My heart pounding, I walked down the aisle toward a microphone and stood in line. I could see Cassie, or rather the back of her head, sitting in the front row, the woman next to her most likely her mom. Three people in line asked questions, and I couldn't tell you what they were about or what my father's answers were. And then suddenly, I was standing in front of the microphone, and the woman was calling on me. She said something about how happy she was that young people were curious, and Keanu nodded yes, isn't it wonderful to see young people here today?

Words just walked out of my mouth, the strange calm of my voice amplified. "I have a comment and a question. You obviously care a lot about seahorses. It must make you feel really good to know that you are helping to protect them."

He smiled. "Yes, it does make me feel good," he said. "We can all help. I hope you'll go to the SOS Web site and check out the resources. There are lots of ways to get involved."

"My question is, how do you feel about the fact

that you abandoned your own child? Do you feel good about that?"

Dead silence.

The flicker of recognition in his gaze.

I didn't flinch. Yes, Keanu, I am your daughter.

The eyes of every person in the auditorium were on me. I turned and walked away, my footsteps silent on the carpet. Someone coughed. I pushed open the door and walked out into the busy aquarium. A family went by, pushing a stroller. I walked around them and ran for the exit.

Outside, the sight of the giant cardboard seahorse, the families streaming up the broad steps, and the beautiful expanse of the lake beyond made me feel even sicker. I yanked the seahorse loose from its sandbag, turned it sideways, and ran down the steps with it.

I struggled against the wind, shifting the seahorse, running past the joggers and families, all the way to the edge of the lake. The wind was cutting across the water, the waves crashing at my feet. I hoisted the seahorse, trying to throw it into the lake, but a gust got under it and slammed it back in my face, pushing me backward onto my backpack. I heard a loud *crack*.

I tore off my backpack and pulled out my uke. The neck was snapped in two pieces, the body cracked, the strings slack.

A yell came from behind, and I turned and saw a museum guard jogging toward me. I left the uke on the cardboard seahorse and took off running.

When I got to the El station, I ran over to a trash can and threw up.

21

KEANU

THERE SHOULD BE a place you can go when you need it. A rip in the fabric of time that you can slip through. It should lead you to a nice room with a bed and a quilt and a little thermos of tea. Maybe a fresh cinnamon roll, a book you can read to take your mind off everything, a recording of your favorite song to play.

I managed to get myself onto a train to Evanston, but I couldn't walk down the station stairs and go home. At that point, I had only two choices: (1) Tell my mom the truth or (2) fake that nothing had happened. Neither seemed possible, so I boarded another train, took it as far as it went, and then returned. Each time the train stopped at my station, I got off, but then I just kept getting onto another train.

After an hour or two, I opened my cell phone. There were messages and texts from my mom, as I knew there would be. Keanu would have called her. *Hey, Pat, just wanted you to know that your darling daughter humiliated me in public. Great job raising her.* Fin and Hayes texted, too, and there were three calls from a number I didn't recognize. My dad? I didn't read or listen to any of the messages.

The sky was darkening with late afternoon thunderclouds. Another hour passed and then another and another, until the streetlights came on. I was so hungry I thought I might faint, but if I left the station, I'd have to pay to get back in, and I was afraid of running out of money. Finally, I got off at LaSalle, found a convenience store, and inhaled a candy bar. I had enough money for one more trip. As I walked back to the station, the rain started, heavy and hard.

Drenched, I got back on the train, leaned my head against the glass, and watched the rain pour. The lights of the shops and cars had that sad, beautiful look they get in the rain, the lengthening reflections of all the colors in the water on the street like long wails of reds, and yellows, and blues, and greens.

The guy behind me asked if I knew the time and when I looked at my cell phone and told him, I realized that the open mic at Ray's was about to start. Hayes must have figured out I wasn't coming.

It was around 7:20 when I got off the train in Evanston and heard my name. Fin's dad rushed up the platform steps. He was wearing a raincoat with the hood up and his big green gardening boots. The lenses of his glasses were streaked with rain. "Min darlin'! We've been looking all over for you."

I did what I'd been doing for the past few hours: I walked over to a bench and sat down. My body had turned into a shell; even though I was soaked, I swear I couldn't feel it. The track was silent, so I looked down and found a cigarette stub to stare at, wedged in the widest part of a crack in the cement.

"Are you okay?"

I felt myself nod.

He joined me, the wet green of his boots coming to rest with a rubbery thump as he sat next to me.

"We split up to look for you. Everybody's worried." He took off his glasses and wiped them on the dry hem of his shirt. "Fin is walking around downtown Evanston. Jenny and the boys are over at your house, waiting in case you come home. Your mom is driving around. She called the police."

My green dress was clinging to my thighs. My left knee was bruised. I wondered where that came from.

"You're shivering," he said. "You're freezing." He took off his raincoat and put it around my shoulders. The flannel on the inside was warm, and it smelled the way Fin's house always smelled — like gingerbread.

His phone buzzed, and he answered. "Yeah . . . She's here . . . she's okay. . . . No, we're just sitting here for a minute. . . . Call your mom, okay? I'm going to call Minerva's mom."

It was Fin. I thought about how he didn't get the part in the play that he wanted, how I wasn't there for him. I pressed the bruise on my leg to see if I could make it hurt, and glued my eyes back on that cigarette butt while Mr. O'Connor called my mom.

"Pat, she's here at Central Station. . . . Yeah . . . she's fine. . . . I can bring her. . . . Okay . . . sure . . . yeah . . .

yeah . . . Okay, see you in a few minutes." He slipped his phone back into his pocket. "She's not far from here. She said to wait."

Mr. O'Connor sat with me on the platform as two trains came and went and as the rain pounded on the station roof; and then my mom came flying up the stairs in her navy blue raincoat, her face colorless, her eyes red. She hugged me and thanked Fin's dad, and we walked down the stairs to the cars.

I tried to give Mr. O'Connor his raincoat back, but he wouldn't take it.

"Bring it next time you come over, darlin'," he said, and I could feel the kindness of his eyes on my face, but I couldn't look at him.

After we got on the road, my mom didn't say a word. I don't know if she was trying to decide what to ask, or what to say, or if she was trying to pretend that nothing had happened. I looked out the window and pressed the bruise on my leg until we arrived home.

Fin's mom and brothers were gone by the time we got there. Mrs. O'Connor had left a note along with a pot of soup and a salad. I thought I would have killed for food, but I couldn't eat. All my mom said was,"You should get out of those wet clothes, Minerva."

I was about to head up to my room, when the knock came.

My mom looked out the security peephole in the door and started saying words I didn't even know she knew.

The knock came again. My dad's voice: "I know you're there, Pat. Open the door."

The room felt charged, like a hurricane was about to hit.

"I will call the police," my mom said.

"Go ahead. We need to have this out," he said.

My mom threw her raincoat back on and rushed out, quickly closing the door behind her. The silence lasted only a second.

"You are not coming inside this house, Keanu."

I walked over to listen.

"Fine. You want to have it out here? Fine — "

"Lower your voice — "

"She inherited all your rage, didn't she? This is my first time seeing her since I left, and this is what I get? I did not deserve this," he yelled.

She screamed: "You left."

"I was right to leave and you know it. We had nothing in common. It was a fling. A mistake. I was young and you threw yourself at me, and I've been paying for it — "

"Oh. It was all my fault? You are so — You're just out for yourself, Keanu. You always were. You can't expect Minerva to forgive you."

"Has she at least heard my side of the story? I wanted her in my life. You're the one who refused."

"What was I supposed to do, Keanu? Put her on a plane to California every other weekend?"

"We could have worked something out if you had tried."

"If *I* had tried? I did what I had to do to protect her. The last thing she needed in her life was an absentee father."

"I didn't want to be one. You forced that issue."

"I forced the issue? You moved two thousand miles away!"

"I was offered a job, a career. You weren't even working! What was I supposed to do?"

"If you really wanted to be a father to Minerva, you

wouldn't have taken that job in California. You would have stayed."

"I might have done that if you were a reasonable person to deal with. You didn't want me in her life even when I was here."

"That is not true. You put your career above everything. I wanted her to have one solid home, not to be torn between two. You were too busy to even think about her."

"I sent her a gift every birthday and I never — "

"What was that supposed to prove? That you love her?"

"What did you tell her about me? Did you tell her that I abandoned you? Is that your story?"

"You did abandon us. You moved away. Leave, Keanu. If you don't, I am calling the police."

"Oh, I'm so sick of this, Pat! You're always the victim! I never missed a payment. I asked you to share custody — "

"Go away! This is my house, Keanu. You have no right to — "

"I paid for this house, Pat. She is my daughter, and I have the right — "

"Stop it," my mom hissed. "I made a life for Minerva here. I gave her love and stability. I took her to the doctor when she got sick. I drove her to school every day and packed her lunch and protected her from — "

"From what? From me? What did you tell her about me?"

"What was I supposed to tell her? How do you explain that to a child?"

"People do it all the time. You were jealous, Pat. You didn't want Minerva to be part of my life because that would have eaten you alive."

"I did it for *her*. She was better off not knowing. She was better off without you. She didn't need to grow up having to visit a father who puts his own needs ahead of hers. If you had really wanted her in your life, you would have tried a lot harder than a gift or two every year."

"I'm sorry, but I'm not going to take parenting advice from you. I obviously could have done a better job raising her than you did."

I stood perfectly still at the door, listening to their voices rage and to the pounding of the rain on the roof, and a cold calm came over me. I walked into the kitchen and around the corner to a little dead-end part of the town house: the utility closet.

A hot water heater was on the left; on the right were an electrical box and floor-to-ceiling storage shelves filled with big, neatly labeled tubs. Three on each shelf. Twelve in all. HALLOWEEN DECORATIONS. CHRISTMAS DECORATIONS. VALENTINE'S DECORA-TIONS. EASTER DECORATIONS. GLASSWARE. HARD-WARE. LIGHTBULBS . . . I started at one end and opened each lid.

When I opened the seventh tub, the one labeled ELECTRICAL CORDS, the strength rushed out of my knees. It was filled with gifts, each one wrapped in birthday paper. Gift after gift after gift after gift — different sizes, shapes, and colors, some with ribbons and bows, some plain — each one with an unopened card tucked under a ribbon or taped to the gift wrap, with *To Minerva* on the front.

The eighth tub, labeled HEATING FILTERS, was filled from bottom to top with more presents.

I sat on the concrete floor, the colors swimming before my eyes. I lifted out a package and opened the card.

Dear Minerva,

Happy eighth birthday. This charm bracelet is from Hawaii. I bought it at a shop that's not far from where I grew up. The woman at the store said it's a kid's size, but if it's too big, you can take out a link or two. Save the links. If you still want to wear it when you're bigger, you can add them back on.

Love, your dad

Stretched out in the narrow white box was a pretty silver bracelet with eight charms, each one enameled with a little splash of color: a blue sailboat, an orange fish, a green hula girl, a red Hawaiian shirt, a pink seashell, and a small brown ukulele. A tiny uke.

I took the bracelet out of the box and laid it across my wrist. It was too small, which meant that it would have probably fit perfectly then. I imagined my eight-year-old self putting it on, marveling at each charm. Balancing it on my wrist, I turned the little uke right side up so the color showed. The four tiny strings, painted white against the brown, were perfectly straight and parallel.

A part of me wanted to cry, a part of me wanted to scream, a part of me wanted to tear open every gift, and a part of me wanted to run away. I reached way down into the tub and pulled one out from the bottom.

Dear Minnyboo!
  You're three! That's so big. I love you and I miss you. Remember our favorite song? This little guy plays it. Take good care of him. I hope to see you soon. Happy birthday!
  Love, Daddyboo

Inside the box, cradled in blue tissue paper, was a stuffed animal — a baby beluga whale — brand-new, snow-white, pillow soft, with a tiny adoption certificate and official-looking gold seal attached to the bright red tag. I wound the gold knob in the middle of the whale's belly and let it go. The tinkling high notes of "Baby Beluga" filled the room, familiar, even though I hadn't heard the song for years.

The gifts, just the sight of them, were starting to make me feel dizzy, as if each one had the power to pull me down a drain hole in time and space.

"Minerva!" My mom's voice flared in the distance. She called for me again, and it lit a fuse of anger inside me. I pictured her all those years, getting those packages in the mail and depositing them into these tubs, deliberately hiding them from me, writing out the false labels, ELECTRICAL CORDS and HEATING FILTERS, so I wouldn't find them. The anger grew hotter at the sound of her footsteps going up the stairs, her voice in my bedroom, her steps coming down again.

"Minerva." She appeared in the doorway, wet from the rain, her hair plastered down on the sides of her face. She looked at the two open tubs, at the gift wrap and the whale, with disbelief and horror.

I rose to my feet, my skin prickling with cold but my blood on fire. "Why didn't you just throw them out?"

She stood there, mascara streaked, speechless.

I erupted. I picked up the full tub and threw it against the wall. The gifts scattered, and she jumped back. I flew at her, my face in her face, my voice burning: "I hate you. I hate him. I hate you both."

I walked past her, stopped in the kitchen, opened the pantry drawer, and got a box of garbage bags.

"Minerva, let me explain. . . ."

I slammed the drawer shut, took the bags to my room, and closed and locked the door.

First things first. Text to Aunt Joan: **Your sister is a pathological liar.**

Next, I pulled out a garbage bag and shook it open. If you could have seen me at that moment, you would have been worried because I wasn't screaming or crying or collapsing onto the floor, which is what you might expect. My anger was there, still red-hot, like embers smoldering under a burned log, but I was focused on a task that suddenly needed to be done. I stuffed the bedspread and matching sheets — pink flowers — into the bag.

I got another bag and walked over to my dresser. I opened a jewelry box that my mother had given me and took out the earrings I had bought at the Goodwill and the ones Fin gave me, and set them aside. I dumped the rest of the jewelry in the garbage bag and then threw the jewelry box in, too. I saved the uke book Fin gave me for my birthday, and the stone Hayes gave me on the beach. Everything else on the top of my dresser went into the trash. I opened each drawer, set aside only the clothes I had bought for myself, and dumped the rest. Two bags full. I opened a chest at the foot of my bed, full of old snow pants and bulky wool sweaters. Baa baa black sheep, have you any wool? Yes, sir, yes, sir, three bags full. I got another bag and walked over to my closet. I saved my Goodwill dresses and threw in everything else, hangers and all. Five bags full, including the snowflake sweater that I had brought home from school back in late January. Happy birthday to me.

I was sweating and shivering at the same time, but I didn't stop. I found a hoodie I had borrowed from Fin and put it on. More bags. In went the vase with the pastel silk flowers and those weird Easter eggs on sticks that my mom had put out after St. Patrick's Day was over, the decorative pillows that were scratchy, the faux antique reading lamp that was hard to turn off and on, the framed tree drawing I did in the second grade and never liked, the stained-glass rabbit with the cutesy smile, hanging on my window.

When I tied up the last bag and opened the door, my mom was sitting on the stairs. She looked up, her eyes puffy and red. I dragged two garbage bags past her down the stairs and left them on the sidewalk in front of our town house in the pouring rain. Then I came back for more. One after another and then another. My mom didn't try to stop me; she just sat there like a zombie. When I had put all the bags outside, I went back into my room and locked my door. I desperately wanted to go into her room and get my winter quilt from Aunt Joan, which was stored under her bed, but I didn't want to see her again, so I put on a dry T-shirt and jeans, curled up on my bed, and tried to get warm.

I heard my mom's cell phone ring. She didn't answer.

In the middle of the night, I woke up sweating but cold. I went to the bathroom and found my mom sleeping on the floor outside my door. The bathroom door was open, a soft orange light coming from the night-light. She sat up, Indian style, and I was struck by how physically small she looked.

"Are you okay?" she asked.

I walked around her and went to the bathroom and got a handful of towels. Back in my room, I closed the door and wrapped myself up in them.

Are you okay? Yeah . . . sure. Not a worry in the world.

22

AUNT JOAN

THE NEXT DAY, my throat was raw and my pillow wet. I stayed in bed all morning and wouldn't answer my mom's knocks. When I went to the bathroom, she snuck in and put white sheets and the "sick blanket" on my bed. It was this plain brown blanket that was easy to wash that my mom always put on my bed when I was sick in case I threw up.

That afternoon, I fell into a woozy kind of sleep, and at one point, I felt her hand on my forehead.

"You're burning up, Minerva," she said.

She drove me to an urgent care center and I believe she was grateful when I tested positive for strep because it gave her something to focus on. She brought me juice and applesauce and medicine, and I still couldn't look at her, so I'd turn and face the bare wall and pretend to be asleep whenever I heard her coming.

I stayed home from school for a few days, and my mom stayed home from work. The home phone rang a number of times, and she whispered a lot, but I didn't care who she was talking to or what she was saying.

Fin and Hayes texted and called, but I didn't answer. Joy called, too, frantically, saying that Cassie had quit and asking if I could work overtime if she could rearrange the party times. I didn't answer anyone. I was beyond vimless.

The antibiotics worked and my throat stopped hurting, but I stayed in bed. At dinnertime on a Wednesday or Thursday, I heard noises at the front door and then in the living room. I tiptoed out into the hallway and was shocked to hear Aunt Joan's voice.

". . . because you obviously both need help, Pat."

My mom: "We're fine, Joan. I don't know why you came all — "

"Minerva's text was a cry for help. What exactly did you tell her about Keanu?"

"Nothing. This isn't about him. Minerva is sick. She has strep."

"It's not just strep. She is self-destructing, Pat, she needs — "

"She is fine — "

"I called him up. I called Keanu. He told me about the whole episode at the aquarium."

"You what?"

"I was worried about you, and you wouldn't talk to me, and I was worried about Minerva, and she wouldn't talk to me. And Minerva had mentioned Keanu to me, so I'm thinking that he must have shown up and done something downright despicable and I called him up to give him a piece of my mind, and we had a very interesting conversation."

"So now you're on his side?" my mom yelled.

"I'm not on either of your sides, Pat. He gave up too easily because his career was more important to him than anything else. He made a huge mistake. But you . . . Pat . . . Did you ever think that maybe that girl should have been allowed to have a relationship with her own father?"

I was holding my breath. Feeling dizzy again, I stepped back from the stairs.

"I didn't do anything, Joan. He was the one who left."

"Pat, did he invite you to Disneyland and not show up, or did you take Minerva out there yourself and then tell us that he didn't show?"

Silence.

Aunt Joan went on. "He said you called when you were already at Disneyland, that he didn't know you were coming, that you had a huge argument because you had a fantasy that once he saw Minerva again, all your troubles with each other would magically disappear. Why did you tell us that he invited you and then didn't show up? So we'd hate him? So we'd feel sorry for you?"

"He did invite us. He said, 'Why do I have to move to Illinois to see Minerva? Why can't you come to California?'"

"That's different, Pat. I think you're twisting — "

"He deserves to be hated, Joan. He would not have been a good fath — "

"Pat, maybe we can find a way to move forward. You can't change what you did, but you can start fresh right — "

"Get out, Joan," my mom yelled. "This is none of your business."

"He is not an evil person. He's been paying child support all along. You can't keep — "

"This is my house and Minerva is my daughter and — "

I closed my eyes. I tried to focus on the wooden floor of the hallway under my bare feet, but I was having trouble. A memory kept flashing through my head. When I was nine, I was at Lake Michigan with Fin and his dad as a storm came in. There was no lightning or rain, just wind, and the waves grew bigger than I had ever seen them. Fin and his dad loved it. They were whooping and hollering, diving into the waves, thrilled at the wild force of the water. I tried to keep up with them. I knew I should swim out to where they were, where it was easier to ride the waves, but instead, I was frozen at the middle point, where the waves were breaking. I kept getting slammed back. Then I saw a huge wave coming, like a monster. I remember the dark green underbelly of it as it rose higher and higher; and instead of diving under it, I panicked, turned my back to it, and tried to run against the outgoing current to the shore. The wall of water crashed over me, dragging me under and spinning me upside down. I thought I was going to die.

"Our family has a tendency to clam up when things get tough, and it's got to stop," Aunt Joan said. "I know you love Minerva more than anything in this world. I love her, too, and I love you, and that's why I'm here. Where is she?"

My feet found the floor, and a sudden breath filled my lungs. I ran down the stairs.

"Minerva!"

They were standing in the living room, my aunt Joan looking like a short and sturdy cowgirl with her round face and curly grayish-brown hair, her jacket still on, a suitcase by the door. My mom's face was white as a stone; she stood, trembling, her arms wrapped around herself, horrified to see me.

"Minerva, honey," my aunt Joan said.

I rushed past them to the utility room and opened the door. Unable to face it, my mom had left everything as it was, the gifts from one of the tubs spilled across the floor, the baby whale and the charm bracelet lying there. I grabbed the full tub, brought it into the living room, and dumped the contents at my mom's feet. An explosion of color, of ribbons and bows, of polka dots, and stripes, and stars, and hearts.

There it was again, the huge wave of anger and sadness coming at me with a force that seemed impossible to withstand. The familiar panic hit and I wanted to turn and run, but I looked at my mom, my throat burning. "You knew it would have been wrong to throw them out, didn't you?" I yelled. "Who would throw away a child's presents, right? But you couldn't give them to me, could you? Because you didn't want me to have the tiniest bit of love for him."

Tears started streaming down my face. I felt like I couldn't breathe, but I kept yelling. "So you did what you always do. You tucked everything away in neat boxes and you labeled it with lies and you hid it. You pretended it never happened. You lied."

My mom put her face in her hands and started sobbing.

"All these years," I cried. "All these years, I thought the reason he left was because I wasn't good enough, or pretty enough, or interesting enough." The tears were running down my neck. "Every birthday party, when my friends had gone home and you were cleaning up, folding all the gift wrap, I was in my room, looking at myself in the mirror and wondering what was wrong with me."

She looked up, her face a mess.

"You weren't protecting me!" I sobbed. "You were hurting me."

She took a step toward me. "Minerva — I'm sorry. I'm so sorry. Please . . ."

I stepped back.

We stood there, staring at each other, my mother, still sobbing, her eyes pleading with me for forgiveness.

Aunt Joan stepped in, crying, too. "It was good to let all that out, Minerva. That was hard, but good. And I'm sure there's more in there. None of this is going to get resolved in an instant." She tried to put her arm around me, and my mom started apologizing again.

I couldn't take it.

I pulled away. "I can't just forget what you did! I will never forget what you did!"

I pictured myself walking out the door and never coming back, and I swear my mom could see into my mind because fear flashed out of her, and the air in the room turned ice cold. I could tell she wanted to step toward me, to hug me, to hold onto me, but she looked afraid to move.

Finally, Aunt Joan broke the silence. "Nobody expects you to forget, Minerva. You have a right to be angry." She grabbed a tissue box and handed us each a handful of tissues. "Here's what I think we should do. Pat, I'm going to make some tea and we're going to sit down in the kitchen together. Minerva, you go upstairs and take a long hot shower and change out of those pajamas you've been wearing all week." She blew her nose. "Then we're going to meet back in the kitchen and we're going to talk some more. We might cry some more, too, and that's all right."

~

IN THE SHOWER, the water washed over me, and I closed my eyes and let all the bad memories come up, and instead of pushing them down, I allowed myself to feel the depth of all that sadness.

23

DEALING WITH WRECKAGE

EVERYBODY THINKS you can't trust teenagers. Adults make mistakes, too. The only difference is that their mistakes are bigger.

You might think that my mom and I talked it out and lived happily ever after or that my dad and I got together and lived happily ever after or that I went to Colorado with my aunt Joan and lived happily ever after, but none of those things happened.

What happens after a major conflict is this: Each minute passes and you begin a whole series of awkward and painful encounters with the people in your life who you can't avoid because they are your family. That night, we began the first of many awkward talks around the kitchen table. My mom, me, Aunt Joan.

Aunt Joan insisted that I needed to talk with Keanu. My mom was terrified and I didn't want to, but Aunt Joan told us a story about a horse on her neighbor's ranch that died because of a festering wound. "This whole thing with Keanu is going to eat away at you unless you deal with it, Minerva," she said. "It's going to take time, and it's not going to be easy, but you can't sit there and let it fester."

Fester. Absolutely great word.

My aunt did the calling right then and there. Keanu said he thought we should all meet in a family therapist's office. My mom started having a fit, but Aunt Joan gave her a look that shut her up, and she agreed to make the appointment. The days ahead, having to deal with my dad and my mom and Cassie and her mom, all of that was like another storm in the distance. I knew it was coming and I dreaded it, but I also knew that I had to deal with it.

I couldn't bring myself to hug my mom or to accept her apology, but I tried to listen to her talk about how much she loved me and how scared she was of losing me.

At some point, exhaustion hit and none of us could talk any more. I dragged myself to my room and closed the door, but I knew it was going to take me a while to settle down.

My room smelled like a sick person. I threw my dirty clothes in my hamper, opened the window a crack to let in some fresh air, and went to my dresser to get socks because my feet were cold. My drawer was empty. The only things on the top were the things I hadn't tossed into those big garbage bags: my phone, a half dozen pairs of earrings, the stone Hayes gave me on the beach, and my birthday present from Fin, the uke book.

I picked up the stone, the book, and my phone and crawled into bed.

Outside my door, I could hear my mom and Aunt Joan saying their good-nights.

After I heard my mom's door close, I called Fin.

"Minerva!" The happiness in his voice almost made me start crying all over again. "I didn't think you'd ever call. Are you okay?"

"I'm alive."

"That's good! Where are you?"

"In my room. My aunt is here." I took a breath.
"Fin, I'm so sorry you didn't get the part you wanted
in the play."

He laughed. "I'm playing a dead townsperson.
I don't even have one line. I stand there in heaven,
choking on my own bile, while I have to watch Jeremy
Kutchins butcher the best scene in the play. I'd kill
myself, but I'm already dead."

I had to laugh. "It sounds terrible, Fin. I'm so sorry."

"When are you coming to school again?"

Suddenly, I wanted to go back, to see Fin's face,
to find Hayes in the hallway, to get on with my life.
"Tomorrow," I said. "I need to get out of here. I need
some Fin vim."

He laughed. "I need some Min vim."

"See you tomorrow."

"Okay."

"I love you, Fin."

"I love you, too, Min."

24

MOVING
FORWARD

SCHOOL WAS STRANGE because I felt as if my entire world had changed and yet absolutely everything was exactly the same. Almost exactly. In U.S. gov, we had moved on to the Industrial Revolution, and in bio, we had moved on to land mammals. Change in content. No change in boredom.

I called Joy. If I really didn't have to deal with Cassie at work, I wanted the job. I told her I couldn't come in that weekend because of my aunt's visit but that I could return the next. "Thank the Lord," she said. "And stay away from the fruity-tooty tanning cream."

Aunt Joan flew back to Colorado on a school day.

I was sad to say good-bye, and I think she was, too, because she gave me a bone-crushing hug. That woman is strong. I guess when you live on a ranch, you don't need to buy workout DVDs to stay in shape.

After school, I arrived home to the hum of the washing machine in our otherwise quiet house. My mom had taken the day off and was doing all the laundry. I grabbed a snack and went up to my room, which was still as bare as a monk's cell, and there on that ugly brown bedspread was a beautiful, brand-new uke, just like my old one.

I picked it up and strummed it.

In the hallway, my mom walked by with a laundry basket.

"Did Aunt Joan get me this?" I asked.

She shifted the load in her arms. "I did," she said.

I didn't know what to say.

She shrugged. "I was dying to buy you a new bedspread, but I'm going to let you pick that out. I have a sneaking suspicion that we do not have the same taste."

I had to laugh.

Her eyes filled with tears and she choked up. She set down the basket and came into my room to hug me.

I felt the rage rising again, but love was there, too, deep inside, and I reached through the anger and hugged her back.

~

THAT NIGHT, I played and sang my heart out.

> This is the bird that flew in the door,
> This is the bracelet that fell on the floor,
> This is the gift that should have been mine,
> This is the heart of the valentine.
>
> Look what the net dragged in.
> Can't throw it back again, again, again.
>   Oh . . .
>
> This is the truth I hold in my hand.
> This is the truth I hold in my hand.
>
> This is the day I needed the charm,
> Tiny and silver to keep me from harm,
> "Love is home," says the painted sign
> Hung by the clock that stopped
>   keeping time.

Look what the net dragged in.
Can't throw it back again, again, again.
  Oh . . .

This is the truth I hold in my hand.
This is the truth I hold in my hand.

This is the mermaid who lives on the land,
Knives in her footsteps and trident in hand.
This is the voice that she wouldn't trade.
This is the wave that couldn't sweep her away,
Sweep her away, sweep her away, sweep
  her away. . . .

This is the truth I hold in my hand.
This is the truth I hold in my hand.
This is the truth I hold in my hand.

25

THE LAST THING

IT WAS HAYES'S birthday. Fin and I took him to Pan Asia Café and I brought cupcakes, so we lit a candle and sang and gave him our present, which was an old paperback we'd found at Bookman's Alley: *Clever and Cool Ways to Avoid Curse Words*. We signed the card *Love, Joy Banks*. Hilarious.

We hung out in town all night. I had my uke, so we did a little busking and made enough money to split a second dessert at Hartigan's.

Fin had to go, but Hayes and I walked over to the

lake. We took off our shoes and walked on the cold, soft sand to the water's edge. All the stars were out and the moon, full and bright, spilled a glow on the lake, rippling a path of white light across the surface. Small waves were breaking lightly right at the edge of the shore.

Hayes picked up a stone and skipped it across the water. Then he waded in up to his knees, not bothering even to roll up his jeans.

"You're insane." I laughed and suddenly remembered his list. "Hey, it's your deadline! Did you do everything on your list?"

He turned back toward shore and looked at me. There was enough light for me to see his face. His hair was longer now, the curls falling in his eyes.

A gentle wave came in, and Hayes raised up on his tiptoes to avoid getting wetter. "I have one thing left."

The wave folded and the foam spread at my feet. "You have to do it," I said. "Tell me what it is."

"I can't tell you the last thing," he said. "But remember how you wanted to know the first thing on the list?"

I nodded.

"I'll show you that." He pulled his folded index card out of his wallet and held it up.

"Just say it," I said.

"No. You have to come out here and read it."

"I'm not coming out there," I said. "The water is freezing."

He shrugged. "The water is invigorating."

Minerva, thy name is Curious. Bracing against the shock of cold, I pulled up my skirt and waded out. He was right. The tingling on the bottoms of my feet was that good kind, when the water is just cold enough to wake up all your cells, to make you feel alive.

Another small wave was coming in and Hayes rose up again on his tiptoes and held the card higher, the white of it almost blue in the moonlight, so that only the top few resolutions were visible. There it was in his neat handwriting, in black ink, above *get a job* and *record some music*:

Say hi to Minerva Watson.

I was speechless.

The wave broke and the tide rushed back out,

stronger than I expected, pulling the sand from under my feet. I stumbled and caught my balance just in time.

He put the list back in his pocket.

"'Say hi to Minerva Watson' was . . . that was on . . . that was the first thing on your list?" I stammered.

"Remember that day I got on the elevator and said hi to you, and Fin joked about how I was stalking you?"

"I do."

He smiled. "I sort of was."

Another wave came, and I braced for the shift in the sand. "Why did you want to say hi to me?"

He took a step closer. "Last semester, I had two classes by your locker, so I kept noticing stuff about you. That poster you had . . . REJECT THE ORDINARY . . . the way you and Fin would sing harmonies . . . the way you shared the locker and would leave each other notes . . . the way you guys made each other laugh . . . the way you yelled at Rick Rogan for giving Fin a hard time. I said to myself, *That girl is interesting.*"

The moon seemed to be glowing brighter, as if someone had turned up the voltage.

"I can't believe you noticed me," I said.

He laughed. "You guys were really loud. You were

impossible not to notice. But I didn't do anything about it all semester. When school started up in January, on that first day back, I heard you singing your tiny violin song in the park after school and you were wearing funny striped leggings and big snow boots, and then you tried to give Fin a piggyback ride and you both fell down in the snow. I tried to find the right moment to say hi at school but didn't. So the day of the audition, I followed you into town, and I kept waiting for you and Fin to say good-bye and walk down separate streets, only you didn't. So I just followed you both into the building . . . and the rest is history."

The sound of people laughing drifted from somewhere down the shore and mixed with the sounds of distant traffic and the leaves of the treetops rustling in the breeze. They were beautiful sounds, all-is-right-with-the-world sounds.

"Okay. I'll tell you a secret," I said. "I wasn't going to audition that day, but then you got on the elevator and you said you were going to do it, so I said yes."

"Because of me?"

I nodded and looked out at the lake. "I said to myself, *That guy is interesting.*"

He smiled. Killer dimples. "Okay. Close your eyes."

"Why?"

"'Cause it's almost midnight and it would be ridiculous to not do the last thing on my list."

"Is the last thing on your list 'Throw Minerva in the lake'?"

He laughed. "No. Close your eyes."

"But I don't want to miss it."

"If you don't close your eyes, you will miss it."

"Okay." I closed my eyes. A small wave crested just over my knees, sending a new chill through me. The wave broke and I could feel the tide rushing out, the particles of sand slipping underfoot, the current trying to pull me off balance again, but I dug my feet into the sand and held on.

"I'm going to do it right now," Hayes whispered.

And then he kissed me.

SOME OF
MY SONGS

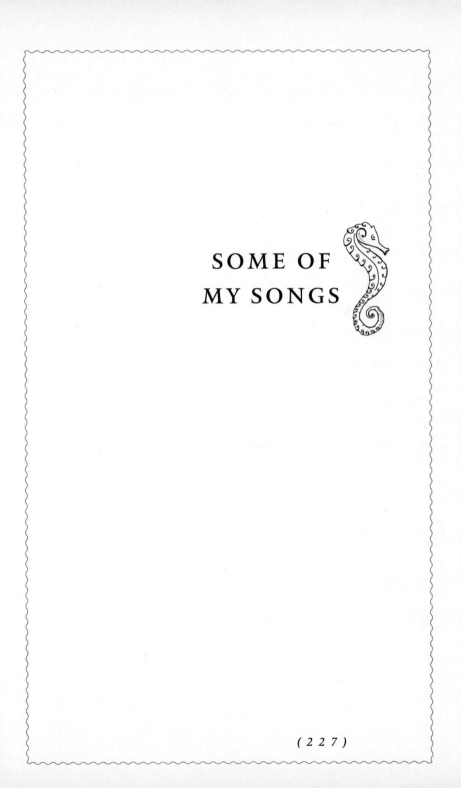

SALT

INTRO
Gsus2
I am the salt
A7
In the water,
C6   G
A far cry from sweet.
Gsus2
I am the salt,
A7
And it's all your fault.
C6   G
I am the salt in the sea.
VERSE
G
You got a boat.
          Bm
Think you own the sea.
G7
Want to sail here
           C
And say hello to me?

A7   D7
You're still a nobody.

CHORUS
G6 Gsus2 C Cm
Don't try to hold me. Oh, no.
G6 Gsus2 C Cm
Don't try to own me. Oh, no.
G6 Gsus2 C Cm
Don't you try to know me.

VERSE
G
Waves throw castaways
    Bm
On the sand:
G7
Broken seashells
     C
And rusted cans—
A7   D7
That's what you mean to me.

REPEAT CHORUS

BRIDGE
    G
And I won't waste time
G7
Thinking of you,
C
Won't chase the tide
    A7
Of that deep and bonny blue.

REPEAT CHORUS

OUTRO

Gsus2
I am the salt
A7
In the water,
C6   G
A far cry from sweet.
Gsus2
I am the salt,
A7
And it's all your fault.
C6   C   Cm
I am the salt in the sea
Gadd9
In the sea.

MONEY

VERSE

A

Don't send me pearls or shiny things,

G

Don't give me any bling.

     F   E

I'm not a girl who likes the tangled strings of debt.

A

Don't give me gifts so I'll forget

G

Mistakes you made, you'll lose that bet.

   F   E

My heart's an iron fist inside my chest.

PRECHORUS

F

Been giving it, giving it, giving it thought. . . .

E

I will not be bought.

CHORUS

A

I got tens and Benjamins,

A

Got 'em from the ATM.

E
Money makes the world go round.
G
Gotta have the ching, ching sound.

VERSE

A
If our roads should intersect,
G
Turn to the right, and I'll go left
F   *E*
Elect to swerve and let's avoid the wreck.
A
Don't think I'll behave the way
G
You want me to. Don't hold your breath.
         F   *E*
You'll get depressed. I'm not some Juliet.

REPEAT PRECHORUS

REPEAT CHORUS

VERSE

A
I'll buy dresses, feather beds,
G
A brand-new house of gingerbread.
         F   *E*
I'll buy the dye and dye my hair bright red.
A
Cash my checks and buy some leather,
G
Velvet gloves for colder weather.

F   E
Buy some love for me and all my friends.

REPEAT PRECHORUS

BRIDGE

A   G   F   G
No, no, no, no,

F
I'm not gonna owe you,

G
Not gonna owe you,

E
Not gonna owe you, oh . . .

REPEAT CHORUS

FINALLY

VERSE
D
Saving my wishes,
        E7
Holding my breath,
          G
Outside that window,
        A
Too broke to take that step.
         D
But now I promise
      E7
To nail the test,
     G
Take the oath to pursue
    A
My happiness. Oooh.
CHORUS
D   G
Finally, I'm right where I want to be.
A   D   A
I'm right where, I'm right where I want to be.

D   G
Finally, I'm right where I want to be.
Bb   D   A
Right where I want to be.
VERSE

               D
Are you that person?
               E7
You know the one
            G
Longing to say out loud
A
What you really want.
             D
You draw a picture,
               E7
Show what you need,
      G
Tape it up on the wall
        A
So everybody sees. Oooh.
CHORUS
D   G
Finally, you're right where you want to be.
A   D   A
You're right where, you're right where you want to be.
D   G
Finally, you're right where you want to be.
Bb   D   A
Right where you want to be.

BRIDGE

G   D
Sing the day, sing the sky,
G   D
Sing the paycheck, sing the hi.
G   D
Drop a dollar in my hat.
E7   A
Nothing better than that.

VERSE (Key change)

B   E
Oh! Hey, people
              F#7
Passing on by,
          A
Consider what you miss
         B
If you keep it quiet.
B
(Don't keep it quiet, don't keep it quiet.)

CHORUS

E   A
Finally, we're right where we want to be.
B   E   B
We're right where, we're right where we want to be.
E   A
Finally, we're right where we want to be.
C   E
Right where we want to be.

SECRETS

VERSE
C6
Look in all the windows
B7
Of the houses on the street.
C6
Pretty people with pretty secrets
B7
Underneath their feet.
C6
Cigarettes in the bathroom,
B7
Smoke trails out like steam.
C6
Close the door so no one
Cm   D
Hears you scream, hears you scream.
CHORUS
G   Bb
I got a secret.
G   Bb
I got a weakness.
G   Bb
Don't want to feel it.

F   D7
Keep it, keep it, keep it secret.

VERSE

C6
My father tiptoed out the door
B7
To never-never land.
C6
My mother gives me gifts that prove
B7
She doesn't understand.
C6
I drop words like bombs online—
B7
That's my evil plan.
C6
No one has to know
Cm   D
Who I am, who I am.

REPEAT CHORUS

BRIDGE

Gm6   D
Behind the friendly eyes,
Gm6   D
Behind the smile,
Gm6   . D
A shadow hides.
            Cm   D7
I wonder why there's got to be a dark side.

REPEAT CHORUS

JUST SAYING

VERSE

```
F        Gm    Am7    Gm
```
I want to make a list
```
F         Gm    Am7       Gm
```
Of all the things I don't want to miss—
```
F          Gm          Gm7-5      C
```
This journey full of sudden turns and twists.
```
F      Gm        Am7     Gm
```
You got one of your own.
```
F      Gm     Am7       Gm
```
Your resolutions down in a row.
```
F           Gm             Gm7-5           C
```
Come on and show me what you wrote, I want to know.
```
Gm                       Am7
```
Someday the writing's gonna fade away.
```
Gm                   G7sus
```
We gotta move before it goes.

CHORUS
```
F
```
Something good, something new,
```
            C7sus
```
Something out of the blue,

(2 4 0)

```
F          Gm      Am7      Gm
```
I may be losing or may be winning.
```
F          Gm          Gm7-5              C
```
While I'm on the solid ground, my head is spinning.
```
F  Gm  Am7          Gm
```
But in a quiet room
```
F          Gm      Am7      Gm
```
I'll find the time to heal the wound,
```
F      Gm          Gm7-5              C
```
Grab a line and hold it tight to pull me through.
```
Gm                      Am7
```
We got to keep this world we're on
```
Gm              G7sus
```
From sinking down too soon.

REPEAT CHORUS

F
Something untried and true,
       C7sus
Something big to see you through,
F
Something long overdue.
       C7sus   C
It could happen to me and you.

VERSE

F   Gm   Am7   Gm
Let's get on the next train,
F   Gm   Am7   Gm
Ride the busy rhythm on through the day,
F   Gm   Gm7-5   C
Watch for signs and let our own rules decide the wa
F   Gm   Am7   Gm
Fate could take you and me,
F   Gm   Am7   Gm
Throw us out on some random street.
F   Gm   Gm7-5   C
Strangers we meet could change our destiny.
Gm   Am7
There are cracks in the sidewalk,
Gm   G7sus
I think they're meant to be.

REPEAT CHORUS

INSTRUMENTAL BREAK

VERSE

F   Gm   Am7   Gm
I'm at the very beginning.

THE TRUTH

VERSE

Cm11   G7sus   Csus4

This is the bird that flew in the door,

G7sus   Cm11   Csus4

This is the bracelet that fell on the floor,

Cm11   Fsus4   F

This is the gift that should have been mine,

Cm11

This is the heart of the valentine.

PRECHORUS

Cm   Dm

Look what the net dragged in.

Eb   F   Gm   Ebadd9

Can't throw it back again, again, again. Oh . . .

CHORUS

Fsus4   F   Fsus4   F

This is the truth I hold in my hand.

Fsus4   F   Fsus4   F

This is the truth I hold in my hand.

VERSE

Cm11   G7sus   Csus4

This is the day I needed the charm,

G7sus   Cm11   Csus4

Tiny and silver to keep me from harm,

Cm11   Fsus4   F

"Love is home," says the painted sign

Cm11

Hung by the clock that stopped keeping time.

REPEAT PRECHORUS

REPEAT CHORUS

BREAK

VERSE

Cm11   G7sus   Csus4

This is the mermaid who lives on the land,

G7sus   Cm11   Csus4

Knives in her footsteps and trident in hand.

Cm11   Fsus4   F

This is the voice that she wouldn't trade.

Cm11

This is the wave that couldn't sweep her away,

Dm   Gm   Ebm

Sweep her away, sweep her away, sweep her away. . . .

OUTRO

Cm11

This is the truth I hold in my hand.

G7sus

This is the truth I hold in my hand.

Gm7-5   F

This is the truth I hold in my hand.

To hear the songs, sing to the karaoke tracks,
and download lyrics and chords, check out
www.thrumsociety.com.

Acknowledgments

I OWE THANKS to Yvonne de Villiers at Luna Guitars for her enthusiasm and support; the booksellers, librarians, teachers, bloggers, and everyone at Egmont USA, Penguin Random House, and Scholastic Book Clubs and Fairs for getting *Guitar Notes*, my first Young Adult novel, into the hands of so many readers; Dr. Amanda Vincent, director of Project Seahorse (www.projectseahorse.org), for information about seahorses for this book; Juliette Zielke, Karen Giacopuzzi, and Maria Adamson for feedback on the manuscript; the musicians who gave comments on the songs or helped on the recordings (see my website for that list); Nancy Gallt and Marietta Zacker for their partnership; Regina Griffin at Egmont USA for her always inspiring editorial questions; and finally, to Ivan, for buying me my first uke and for being a holdfast for me even when the waves are strong.